When
Karma
Goes Upside
Down

When
Karma
Goes Upside
Down

DISHANT HURIA

Srishti
PUBLISHERS & DISTRIBUTORS

SRISHTI PUBLISHERS & DISTRIBUTORS
Registered Office: N-16, C.R. Park
New Delhi – 110 019
Corporate Office: 212A, Peacock Lane
Shahpur Jat, New Delhi – 110 049
editorial@srishtipublishers.com

First published by
Srishti Publishers & Distributors in 2017

The novel is dedicated to the misery and sadness I had gone through. Had I not seen the stretch of darkness, I would have never understood the role of karma in shaping up our destiny.

Also thanks to the cigarette brand Benson & Hedges for keeping my anxiety in check during vulnerable times.

Ridhima

Sunday, 15 February 2015

"Why would you not answer my call?"

"Well I was busy... I hardly had time to check the phone," she said.

"Busy enough that you forgot that your boyfriend would be waiting for your call?"

"Yes, kind of!"

I could sense her turning cold. I hung up, hoping she'd call me later and apologize.

The next morning, I received a message from her,

I think we need to take a break. Nothing is going right between us.

I replied, *Well there is no coming back if it is over. Then let it be.*

However, after a couple of hours, I knew I had to put my ego aside. A break up was the last thing I wanted.

So I called her, and when she finally answered, I said, "Ridhima, I want to see you."

She said, "Well, I am out with my friends; it's not possible for me to meet you..."

"Please Ridhima, we've got to talk it out."

"I told you, I need a break. How else do I say it?" She sounded impatient. I could hear music in the background and wondered where she was.

"Well, can you at least meet me once?"

"Fine, I'll be home in an hour. Let me know once you reach. I will come down."

Her voice still had the potential to make me feel weak. Irrespective of the rift, I loved her. I made my way to see her, parking the car right underneath her house. Her flat was on the second floor; I looked towards her balcony and called out loudly from the car, "Ridhima, I am waiting downstairs!"

After about five minutes, I saw her walking towards the car. She had a big smile on her face, as if nothing had happened. She was dressed to kill, and had make-up on her face. I looked at the rear view mirror and ran my fingers through my hair as she entered the car.

She smelled good. I wanted to take her in my arms, but stopped myself. She needed to first set my mind at rest.

I asked her, "What's wrong, Ridhima? Have I done something wrong? Please tell me how I can fix it... we were supposed to be together for a very long time... how come a little hiccup has turned our relationship so fragile?

"Aarush, I cannot feel anything! I have turned numb. I just don't know what's going on," she said, fidgeting with her hands.

"What do you mean, Ridhima? You are not alone in this relationship. I deserve a fair chance. What happened to all those commitments and promises that we made to each other?" I ran my fingers through my hair again, this time in agitation. "Were they meaningless? Weren't we supposed to stay together in the toughest of times? Weren't we supposed to bring new light in our lives, together, with each other?"

"Aarush, I have nothing to say, I am sorry," she said.

"Ridhima, I know you are angry and frustrated with your life. Sitting at home and doing nothing can bring frustration and anguish in anybody, but this does not mean that you should vent it out on our relationship. I have also struggled along with you, haven't I?"

Her face had turned blank, her body language was making it evident that it was over, but my heart was not willing to accept it. I had never been able to give up on anything. I knew my self-esteem would not permit me to let her go so easily. At least she was talking to me.

She said, "Aarush, after all that we have gone through, I know that your love has also faded. It is not the same... and you know it very well."

Maybe she was right, but I hardly had time to think about it. I was more concerned about our future together. I tried to console her and take her in my arms, trying to remind her of how it felt. But she pushed me away. "I don't love you anymore, why don't you get it?"

I could always predict her next move, that's what I had thought ever since I had known her. Four years was a long time. But her present behaviour was unpredictable and rather shocking. I looked at her and felt hollow. She had been the only one right aspect in my life.

And then she said, "I will take your leave now, you better take care of yourself, and it was nice knowing you, Aarush."

Was she talking to a stranger or to me? I did not know what to do or say as she left.

It had been like a melodramatic scene which happened in romantic movies, or so I had thought. Similar movie scenes started playing before my eyes and I started to laugh loudly. I was angry at myself. How could somebody like me lose control over this situation? I was not supposed to feel this way. I switched the car ignition on, took a u-turn and began the thirty-minute drive back from Rajouri to my house in Rohini.

I crossed the first red light, and seeing traffic ahead I presumed it would take no less than forty-five minutes to cross the second light, so I rolled the window down. I could hear honking and abuses on the road and see eunuchs asking for money from the truck drivers. I took out a cigarette and lit it and started to play with the lighter, when my brain started to develop a theory. She had a perfect window: her internship was going to keep her busy for more than fourteen hours a day and there were a lot of happy faces in a radio channel. When you see happy faces, you tend to forget what sadness is all about. Moreover, they were much more confident than I was under the current circumstances, so she would hardly have time to think about me. I parked the car in the not so empty parking lot right underneath my apartment and took the stairs up home.

Sunday, 22 February

Ridhima hadn't called or messaged me for the past one week. We were supposed to celebrate our fourth anniversary today, I thought on my way towards the grounds to play cricket. Considering the loop I was stuck in, I badly needed some confidence, and cricket was just another way of regaining some of the lost self-respect. As I reached the grounds, I could see some sardars standing on one side. All of them had fat bellies and some of them had tattoos on their arms which said, 'Khalsa rules!'

I bowled the first ball of the match and was hit for a six. The guy with the fat belly who was batting looked at me as if he had just won an Oscar. I bowled the next ball at a much better speed and he tried to cut the ball on the off side. The fielder at the gully caught the ball. The batsman walked out with his face down in shame, and I had a loud laugh.

The game continued and I managed to have an impressive wicket tally of five wickets. Walking back, I had a smile on my face. I knew it would only stay with me for a few minutes, but I still enjoyed it.

We won the match, and putting my feelings aside, I went to meet all the sardars that comprised the opposite team, greeting them in a polite manner.

On my way back, I stopped at a nearby panwadi and picked up some cigarettes of my regular brand, Benson and Hedges. I made a call to Ridhima, and she answered instantly.

"Hi Ridhima," I said. "Is there any chance of seeing you today?

"Umm, okay. I will be there at your place in around an hour," she said.

I went home, had a shower, brushed my hair, trimmed my beard, and wore a white t-shirt, ensuring that my chest muscles were visible, and a pair of denim jeans, wanting to look decent enough to meet my girlfriend. After all, appearances did matter.

I went out and saw her sitting in her car. I walked towards her car and she waved at me. I waved back, crossed the road, and sat inside.

"So, how are you, Ridhima?" I asked her, suddenly at a loss for words.

"I am good, Aarush. Where should we go?" She was polite as well.

"We can park the car at an isolated place, sit and talk, if you are fine with it?"

"Yes, I am fine with whatever you want," she said and shrugged her shoulders.

She parked the car next to a movie hall nearby. There was silence for a couple of minutes.

I said, "Let's give one hour to each other to talk and decide..."

She laughed a demonic laugh. A sudden chill went up my spine.

"What's wrong, Ridhima?"

"What should I say? There is nothing much to talk about, is there?"

"Say what is on your mind."

And so the conversation began.

She said, "I told you earlier as well, I do not feel anything anymore."

I looked at her. "And you are realizing this after four years? At least tell me what I have done wrong?"

"Not many, just some small instances that have made me move away from you..."

"But you never told me anything." I was surprised by her words. "We could have tried to turn things around."

"How could I have told you anything, when I was also not sure what was going on?"

"Ridhima, is breaking up the solution?"

"No, it is not." She clutched the steering wheel. "But I don't love you anymore, so how can I be with you?"

I burst out in anger, yet I tried to control the volume of my voice, "Fine, Ridhima. I cannot force you into anything, but please make sure you stick to your decision. I do not have a switch in my body that can go on and off as per your convenience."

I pushed open the car door and stormed out. She called out to me, "Don't leave, I'll drop you home…"

"You have already dropped me, I can get up on my own," I yelled back at her. I started walking back, laughing loudly at myself. Passers-by looked at me in amazement as I walked past the main market in Rohini.

After ten minutes, I received a message from her:

You don't love me in the same manner as you used to. It is not entirely my fault.

I wanted to reply. I wanted to say:

Yes, I do not love you in the same manner. I have changed. People grow. Maybe my love is also different, but that does not mean I do not love you, or my emotions are not as selfless as they use to be. My priorities might have changed, but love is still love. Trying to weigh somebody's emotions is an act of foolishness.

But I resisted this impulse. I knew nothing good would come out of showing my weak side to a woman who had already left me.

The next morning, I got up with a dry mouth. My head was hurting and there was a niggling ache right where my heart was. I headed towards my mother's room. My father was ready to leave for office, and I waited for him to do so. We hadn't been on talking terms for some time. As soon as he left, I went straight to my mother and hugged her, trying hard to control my tears.

Surprised to see me like that, she asked, "What happened, Aarush? Is everything fine? Answer me, son.

As she held me in her arms, I started sobbing. I had no intention to create a scene, but the tears would not stop. She looked a little worried, but I was already feeling a little better. The previous evening's disappointment had made me feel hollow.

My mother asked me, "What's wrong, Aarush? Please tell me."

I said, "I should not have done it."

"What did you do?" she asked, her eyes widening with shock.

"Ridhima... I should have never fallen in love with her! I was wrong about her."

She seemed less worried as I spoke. She must have thought that I had borrowed money from someone, and was now unable to repay it. In a middle class family there is mostly one major problem, and that is Maya, money. Everything seems to be centered around money, and the other emotions do not appear to exist. But I needed someone with whom I could share my emotional pain, and so I did.

My mother consoled me, saying, "It's all right, it will pass in no time. This happens. You may have a heavy heart, but there is nothing much you can do. Just do not have any hatred for her. It is part of a process. You meet people and then they leave. They come into our lives to teach us some kind of lesson."

It was interesting to see how easily she was saying all this, considering the fact that she hated all my paternal family, from my grandmother to my father's sisters. She hated all of them, and anybody who was even remotely associated with them. And 'hate' is a weak word. Given a knife and liberty, she might not think twice before stabbing them all.

I asked her, "I know you are right, but how could I have been so foolish not to see this coming?"

"Well, sometimes we forget, and then we commit mistakes. You've got to stay strong, Aarush, and remember this lesson for the rest of your life."

Days just passed by. I had stopped taking my cellphone to office and preferred staying away from it. I felt that it would help me move on, or relieve me from the pain. But the moment I returned from office, I would rush to the mobile phone, leaving everything aside, hoping she might have called, hoping she still loved me, and believing things would be back to normal. But there was nothing. She had turned cold, like a deep-frosted chicken, and I believe the symptoms of depression were apparent in me now. I could feel the pain, but there was nothing much I could do. I had lost the energy to pick the parts of my heart and sew them together.

One such day, I felt that talking to another girl might help me get away from these feelings so I messaged one of my batch-mates from my language course. She always seemed to be a kind and approachable soul. She was about five feet five inches tall; her body was voluptuous and her smile was delicious. Her name was Radhika, pretty close to Ridhima in sound as well.

It was around 8.00 p.m. when I messaged her,

I was just passing your locality, so I thought of messaging you.

How do you know where I stay? You never asked for my address, she replied.

It's on your Facebook profile. I carried on.

Have you been stalking me? she reverted.

That is information on the internet. Do not reveal it, if you do not want people to know.

Just kidding, what are you doing here in Vasant Kunj? she texted, and I heaved a sigh of relief.

Came here for some office work, on my way back home.

Where do you work? How come you never told me anything about yourself, and now a message all of a sudden? I had managed to raise some curiosity, I thought.

Meet me somewhere for a date and I shall reveal everything. I gave it a good shot.

Well, sounds good to me. She was interested!

Tomorrow 7.00 p.m.?

Sounds good.

I will see you then. I sent the final message.

The next evening, I picked her up and we both went to a rooftop bar in Vasant Kunj. The air was chilly, quite unexpected in early March in Delhi. I was shivering a little but she looked rather comfortable as we settled ourselves on the cane chairs. I ordered a Vat69 large on the rocks and she ordered a beer.

She broke into a smile. "Well, before we start drinking, I would like to tell you something."

"Go ahead," I said.

"When I get a little tipsy, I dance to seduce a man, any man."

My eyes widened. "Okay, that is something new. I have never heard someone make such a confession."

"I know, so I would rather not drink too much."

"That's your call, whatever sets you rolling," I said.

It was a disappointing signal but despite her proclamation, we did end up having a good time. I was four drinks down, so I casually asked her when she needed to be back home.

"Around midnight," she said.

I checked the time. It was 10:15 p.m. I asked the waiter for the check and we left.

In the car, I played some classic rock but realized it was not to her taste. Eventually I mustered up enough courage to ask her, "Would you like to go my flat in Dwarka? You can see peacocks there and we can share some drinks before calling it a day." Though I stayed with my parents in Rohini, I shared this flat in Dwarka with my buddy Nikhil, for rendezvous like these.

She was little hesitant, but said yes.

All this time while driving, I was least bothered about what was running in her mind. I just wanted to have meaningless sex. My room was on the fifth floor, and there was no lift. I knew she would be a little out-of-breath after climbing the stairs, so I climbed first and opened the door. To my surprise, the bed sheets were crumpled, as if somebody had been sleeping on the bed. In the darkness I could make out the beer bottles, empty chips packets and cigarette butts on the floor, so I refrained from switching on the light. I had a zero watt bulb in the room, and I switched it on as she entered the room. I was filled with lust and went a little closer to her and offered her a cigarette.

"Do you like the view?" I asked. "The international airport is hardly two kilometres away; you can see the runway from the balcony."

"I want a room like this someday," she said with a sigh.

I moved closer to her, sitting on the bed's edge. The blue light falling on her face acted as a catalyst. There was definitely some heat between us. She held my hand firmly. I bent my face towards her and kissed her; it was a tender kiss and she responded with a tender moan. In no time, we started to undress each other, and I lifted her boobs with both my hands and licked them. She bent down and I was just on the verge of having what might have been the best blowjob of my life when we both heard the sound of an alarm going off. Shocked out of our state of mind, we started to look for the source of the alarm.

"There is a watch somewhere on the bed," she said. "It's 12:15 a.m. I must leave!"

I cursed my friend Nikhil for the crumpled bed, for leaving his watch behind and for ruining my night. Both of us got dressed hurriedly and then left for the car.

She said on the way, "Let's continue our session next time." I smiled, dropped her at her apartment, and left.

Deepali

It was around two at night after I dropped Radhika home. On my way back, as I lit another cigarette, I could see a red light ahead. I started to decrease the speed of my car and within the fraction of a second I heard a loud noise; it sounded like an explosion. I braked hard and stopped and looked towards the left. There was a guy lying on the road, and then I heard a loud cry of a woman. The tyre of the guy's bike was running freely and heading towards the direction of my car!

I pulled over my car quickly into the side lane and got out to help the boy. A lady came running out of the other car that had also stopped. It must have been her cry that I had heard. She seemed to be in her mid thirties. Her legs were trembling, and it was difficult to make out whether she was drunk or frightened. I carefully opened the cover shield of the boy's helmet. His face was bleeding and he seemed to be unconscious. No one else was around, apart from the barking dogs.

I asked the lady, "Can you call someone for help?"

"Yes, yes, I will, I will," she said, and ran towards her car.

I placed the boy's head in my lap and slowly started removing his helmet. His face was covered with pieces of glass and blood. I tried to wake him up, but he seemed lifeless. The lady came running towards me and said, "I have called for an ambulance and they will be here in some time."

I said, "Well, I don't know how much time we have... we better take him to the hospital on our own."

We managed to lift the heavy guy and got him inside the car and drove towards the nearest hospital.

"Did you see what happened?" I asked her.

She said, "I don't know how this happened. I guess he was driving really fast. His bike lost its balance on one of the potholes on the road and he landed right in front of my car..."

She started crying as soon as she finished.

"I think you should call your family members, the police might interrogate you," I said.

She panicked even more and started to cry even louder.

I took out my phone and called the police and gave them the necessary information.

As we reached the hospital, I immediately rushed towards the ward boys. They ran towards the car, pulled the boy out and took him straight inside the emergency room.

After fifteen minutes, the doctor came to meet us.

He said, "The boy is now gaining consciousness."

We were relieved. There had however been a lot of blood loss and the point of concern was whether there were any internal injuries too.

He said, "If there are only minute internal injuries then he will be on his legs in a few days, but we will get to know this only after all the tests are conducted."

I went out of the ER into the hallway towards the reception. A guy patted me on my back, "Excuse me, which way is the ER?"

He looked calm and sounded polite. I gave him directions and went towards the reception. When I returned, the lady was standing with the same gentleman.

I asked her, "What is the status?"

She said, "Well, he is conscious now, let's see what happens. Do you know where he lives?"

I said, "The police will be looking into it."

It was time for me to leave, so we exchanged numbers. I told her to call me if she needed any help, and left towards the parking lot. As I entered my car, I could smell blood. I lit a cigarette, turned the windows down and drove homewards.

The next day I woke up in the afternoon, with the vision of the incident of the previous night circling in my head. I washed my face and checked my cell phone. There were three missed calls from the lady from the previous night's incident. I returned the call to find out what she had to say.

"Hi Aarush," she said, and her voice sounded quiet and soothing.

"Hey, I hope everything is fine?" I asked her.

"Yes, I mean, his leg is fractured and he has bruises on his body. His family came in early morning...so I left. I guess he will be back on his feet in a month or so."

"Well, good to hear that."

"I just wanted to thank you for yesterday."

"Oh! It's all right," I said.

"Well, if you had not had been there, I would have probably left him there and ran away..." she said and paused.

"Well, not to worry now... I guess luck was in his favour."

"All right, you take care of yourself," she said, and we bid each other goodbye.

I went to my room and took out my sociology books. The entrance tests were approaching and I started to search for a random topic. What opened before my eyes was the Theory of Suicide by Durkheim!

Damn! This was the last thing I wanted to read then, so I started flipping the pages again and kept on doing this aimlessly for an hour or so before my thoughts began to wander.

I realized I had not even asked the lady's name and just saved her mobile number as 'The Lady'. I Googled her number, and found that her name was Deepali.

"A pretty name, indeed," I said to myself, and then Goggled her pictures. There were photos taken in Malaysia, at Universal Studio, in Switzerland, and many other places. She kind of looked single, but her Facebook status said 'married'. I wanted to call her, but it was a complicated call to make, for a number of questions were juggling in my mind. Was she divorced? Did she have a kid?

I went to a nearby restaurant for late lunch. As I returned and started fucking my head with sociology theories again, I received a missed call from Deepali.

I called her, saying, "Hey, I received a call, what's up?"

"I am sorry to bother you... do you know any good mechanic around? I need to get my car checked."

"Where do you stay?"

"Paschim Vihar, Block B."

"Sure, please note down the number." I thought again and said, "Or rather, I'll ask the mechanic to give you a call."

"Thanks again, Aarush."

It was a green signal for me to go ahead, I thought. I immediately called the mechanic and gave him her address, and said to myself, "Wait for the right time to make the next move."

I went to change my clothes to go to the gym. It had become impossible to study.

It was at two in the morning the same night that I was sitting on my desk, waiting for another customer to call and ask questions like how could he possibly fix his computer, there were so many viruses in it, etc. I was working at night, for our company provided computer technical support to Americans, and my job was to turn the call into a sales call. It was not a fixed job, and I was working on commission basis – seventeen percent of the total sales. Let's say, I make a sale of three hundred dollars, I would earn around three thousand rupees.

The money was good, but the profile was not. I was sitting in a cabin that could sit about ten people. The air conditioner was working, but there was no remote, so if we felt cold we had to either switch it off and bear the heat... or bear the cold. Most of the people sitting inside the cabin were either dumb, illiterate, or miserable in their lives. There was nothing good about the office except independence, for I had no fixed working hours and I was not answerable to anyone.

However, most of the Americans who called were old, and it would get really difficult at times to deal with them.

So I sat waiting for a call, reading a book. While reading the book, a sense of isolation overcame me. I had nobody with whom I could share my emotions, and nobody with the potential to understand me. It was getting difficult for me to sustain myself in the office or anywhere else.

Fuck happiness, even peace was nowhere to be found.

Just then, I received a call on my extension. I automatically went into the call mode.

"Thank you for calling technical support. My name is Aarush. How can I help you today?"

"I want you to get out of my computer," said an apparently old agitated man. There was some pop-up advertisement that flashed on his computer and he was unable to remove it.

I said, "Sir, can you please tell me the problem you are facing right now?"

"My hitch is you bastard, scamming people from a third world country! Why don't you get a real job and make a decent living in your life?" His voice was filled with frustration.

Maybe this was how Americans look at us and were not even close to. They were so filled up with the life they led in their privileged society that they were far away from understanding the problems of a person who stayed in India.

I responded, 'You fucking retard, you cannot get rid of an advertisement in your computer and you are blaming an entire country for your failure to solve a simple setback. Why don't you go back to school and learn how to run a computer or maybe something meaningful!"

I hung up and the guy sitting right next to me looked at me in astonishment. I generally do not respond this way to anyone, but that day was different. I was filled with anger and fury, not because of the American, but because of Ridhima.

I took a cigarette and came out for a smoke, thinking smoking might release some pain. I felt far away from reality. I lit my cigarette, then rushed towards my car, and headed towards Ridhima's place. I had no clue why I was doing this; maybe I was not the one in the driver's seat. I parked the car outside her apartment, on the road from where her balcony was visible.

I took a cigarette and stepped outside the car. The road was dark. I knew in which direction her balcony was, but it was not visible.

I asked myself, "What the hell am I doing here?" But I knew I wanted to talk to her. I wanted to tell her that nothing was right, and that I wanted to be with her. But it was not possible.

I searched for my cell phone in the dashboard of my car, and dialled her number. No answer. Finally after the third time I tried, she answered in a sleepy tone. "Hi," she said.

"I am standing underneath your balcony, can you come down?"

"Why are you here?" She paused and said, "Wait, give me two minutes."

I heard the gate open. I could barely see her, but I could sense her.

She said, "What are you doing here?"

I said, "I know you don't want me to be here. I just could not stop myself, I am sorry."

"Don't be sorry, it's all right," she said, running her fingers through her hair. "How are you?" she asked.

"I am good. I got into Pune University. Do you want me to leave?" I asked her.

She said after a pause, "I want you take admission in a good college."

Her voice was firm and strong. She knew what she was saying.

"How are you?" I asked.

"Well, I am good. The internship is good, the people are good. I have started enjoying my work. These people are very creative. I really enjoy their company."

My legs began to tremble. I said, "It's good to know you are happy."

"Yeah, I finally know what I want to do."

"Okay, I will leave now," I said, stubbing the cigarette with my shoe.

"You drive safe," was all that she said.

Anniversary

$\mathcal{J}$t was our anniversary on 22 February. It was our second one. At 11:45 at night I was waiting for her on her rooftop.

There were no lights on her roof and it was dark. I switched on my mobile phone torch to find a place to sit. I had asked her sister to send her on the roof at midnight on some pretext. I had bought a bouquet of red roses and some scented, oval-shaped light brown candles. I was excited, for she loved surprises.

At midnight, the door opened with a grating sound, and she was there. I went towards her. She looked frightened for a second, but then she smiled. I could see the happiness on her face. Her eyes were shining, and her lips had never looked more inviting. Wearing shorts and a blue tank top, she looked ravishing. I put my arms around her waist, bent forward a little and kissed her hand.

"Congratulations, we made it," I said.

She had tears in her eyes. I had never seen her so happy. "I love you Aarush, thank you for everything," she said.

We hugged. I could feel music in the air as we circled around like ballroom dancers. Finally, we sat down in a corner. She whispered, "I love holding your hand. I love resting my head on your shoulders. I love everything you do. Aarush, don't you dare leave me. I promise I will never leave you."

We kissed. I was eating her strawberry lip balm, her hands on my back. We looked into each other's eyes. It was time for me to leave.

We had a date the next evening. I could see her smiling face and how she was blushing. She kissed me again on my cheeks. I said bye to her and walked down the stairs slowly and very carefully, like a thief.

I got inside my car, looked for my cigarettes, and began to play Elton John's 'Rocket Man' as I started for home.

I was about to go to bed when I thought of writing her a letter. The room was dark, but I did not turn the lights on. I started typing the letter with a little help I got from the laptop screen.

> *Hi babe,*
>
> *You wanted me to write something for you.*
>
> *I don't really know what to write, but I am writing something that I may regret in the future.*
>
> *That's right. Because I don't know what kind of future it will be, so I am always scared to tell you something or to react in a way that may make me fall in love with you till infinity. Ridhima, I am a very ordinary person. I have done some terrible things and committed unforgivable mistakes. I struggle every day as a person and find it difficult, most of the times, to handle situations.*

And you were also a pure mistake in my life. I am sorry to say this, but that is the truth. I felt no attraction towards you. Really, I just went with the flow. You came into my life when I never wanted anyone...when I was certain that I didn't need anyone. In short, you entered my life and it was a perfect storm.

You were someone whom I tried with all my force and energy to go away from, but the moment you ignored me, I would begin to shake. The constant effort to get away from you made me fall in love with you. Whenever I asked for you to leave me and you replied with, 'Ok, I will not disturb u', this particular message would send shivers down my spine. The thought that you may really leave me would make me sweat and my heart would begin beating at a faster pace.

In those particular moments, when I used to fight with you, I kept falling for you, and it got impossible for me to stop loving you.

I always say to you, "This is not how I pictured my girlfriend would be". To be honest, you are tough and high maintenance. It is not easy to be with you and match up to your expectations. And now I can say that you may not be the one who I used to picture as my partner, but you are the one I want to be with for the rest of my life. You are tough but I have never liked anything easy. I love it that you are complicated because then I want to unravel your complications, smoothen the knots. I know you still think that you have not understood me, but trust me you know me now.

*And another thing that I wish to take the
liberty of saying…I don't like it when you make any
extraordinary efforts. I can see that you get completely
nervous and under-confident in front me. Believe me,
everything else that you may feel that I don't like are
actually things and habits that I love in you. I love
the manner in which you have loved me. I don't know
whether I can do that and that scares the hell out me.
But Ridhima, I will never stop loving you.*

*I have a feeling that if I lose you, I may be lost
in the crowd. Because I know that no matter what
happens, you will be there with me. Believe me or not,
but my life revolves around you now.*

I love you, Ridhima, now and forever.

My thoughts were wandering to the past, but they had to
return to the present, I was on my way to office, remembering
the outline of the first letter. I was really lost in the crowd;
I was lonely and I wanted her to hold my hand and tell me
that everything would be all right. But the fact was that
there was no 'we' any longer.

I was alone and I had to sail the drowning ship alone.
The moon was shining in its full glory and the tide was high;
the shore was not far although there was still a substantial
distance to be covered. I knew I would make it in the end,
but it somehow felt like a never-ending ride. I thought,
maybe god is punishing me for my wrong deeds, maybe
whatever chaos I have landed into is for a reason, maybe
I am being taught a lesson…I had no clue. There were

too many maybes, and I had an answer to none. All these thoughts entangled my mind and I felt chained.

I heard a constant honking behind me on the road. I glanced at the rear view mirror. The driver seemed to be in a real hurry. Ha, at least this fellow had a purpose, I said to myself, and made way for him to overtake my car.

When I reached office, these thoughts were still playing havoc on my mind, but I managed to greet everyone with a smile. I sat facing my computer and Googled the symptoms of depression:

Disturbed and restless sleep
Problem in concentrating on daily chores of life
Headache
Anxiety
Low self-esteem

How to cure depression:
Consult a psychiatrist
Eat healthy
Exercise and meditation

A psychiatrist could not help me. I was smart enough to know this. I was not going to take any pills for sure. This was a phase and the day I got admission into a decent college, I would be back on my feet. After all, there were so many things that I needed to do – my desire to travel had not died and my thirst to seek knowledge was still alive. I was just short of cash.

The extension rang, and I answered, "Thank you for calling technical support. My name is Aarush. How may I help you today?"

It was one in the morning when I cracked a four hundred dollar sale, and made four thousand rupees, which was decent for the day. I sat on my computer and was filling my sale sheet when my phone beeped.

Hi. It was Deepali.

Hi Deepali. I replied.

Hello, why are you up so late?

I was up preparing a presentation. I work late. It's morning in America, you see. I showed off, subtly.

What work do you do?

Sales for Microsoft products, I extract money from fools.

You are a scammer. :D she replied.

Who isn't, Miss?"

That's true.

You sound like a hardworking woman as well; working this late at night requires passion. I coaxed for more information.

Yes, I love my job. I work for Hindustan Unilever as the Regional Manager.

I wanted to meet her, so I took the plunge, *Meet me for a coffee someday?*

Sunday evening?

I am up for it, I said, exhilarated all of a sudden.

My mind was moving like the piston of a heavy-loaded truck. Her message at night raised a lot of questions for me. Why would a woman in her mid-thirties message me late at night? I needed answers. I was losing patience but I controlled my thoughts and decided to wait till Sunday.

Another call rang, and I answered mechanically, "Thank you for calling technical support. My name is Aarush. How may I help you today…"

❖

It was a typical Saturday afternoon, and I was sitting on a cold bench right in the centre of the park near my apartment with my sociology book and my laptop. I could see some homeless children on the swings. It was a rather hot day and though I was sweating, I needed to smoke. Smoking at home was not a luxury that I could afford, so I lit a cigarette and started reading Karl Marx and labor theory when my cell phone beeped.

Tomorrow, 7 p.m.? Deepali messaged.

She had been out of the picture since the last three days. I had forgotten we had a date on Sunday.

Sure, I'll pick you at 6:30?

Fine, looking forward to it. :)

So am I. I'll call you tomorrow afternoon.

Okay.

I should have been happy. I was going on a date with this woman – mature and experienced. I had always dreamed about finding a woman like her. But despite all that, I was feeling numb. I had lost the energy to meet new people. I was too absorbed in my own loop.

But it was a good opportunity. My rational mind was not permitting me to lose a date with Deepali. I was done with my cigarette and began to walk back home, thinking about why I was filled with this degree of pessimism.

On Sunday evening, I woke up after a nap and called Deepali. "Hey, how are you? I took a nap, sorry for calling so late."

"Oh, it's all right, let me give you directions to my place, see you at 6:30," she said, and proceeded to give me directions to her place at Paschim Vihar.

I showered, trimmed my beard, and headed towards my wardrobe. A white shirt was a safe bet, always. I got my jeans out and got dressed. I applied wax on my hair, and sprayed Dunhill perfume. Both had been gifted to me by Ridhima. I laughed, thinking of how life played ping-pong with you.

We reached Café Coffee Day at Hotel Taj Palace. She was wearing a blue, long-sleeved suit. Her earrings were long, and her black eyes were outlined with kajal.

We took a seat at an outdoor table. It was dark, and a yellow bulb hung on top of us. It seemed to me as if I was here for an interrogation. We ordered coffee and pancakes. I leaned back and asked her, "Who was the guy who came to meet you at the hospital?"

"My cousin, he has gone back to America now," she said.

"Okay, so you stay alone?"

"Yes, my husband passed away seven years ago."

"Sorry to hear that," I said rather surprised.

"It's okay. I don't miss him that much now."

I asked her then, "Any children?"

"No, he passed away way too soon. But he left me his house, and his parents wanted me to stay here. They stay in Dehradun."

I changed the subject. "So where were you coming from so late at night that day?"

"I could not sleep that night, so I decided to go for a drive. I had no clue that the fellow would bounce right in front me. I just wanted to see how Delhi looks at night…"

I shook my head, "Well, you don't really know how or when reality hits you. You may be careful, but life always has a way of amazing you. I know, for I too have been amazed by my life. I can certainly visualize how it must have been for you."

"No, you cannot," she said, taking a bite of the pancake.

"Can I ask you something? What made you message me that night?"

"I don't know. I was just thinking about the incident and I messaged. I hope I did not give out a wrong signal?"

"No, you did not. I am too dumb to understand signals. I get confused between right and left, so I prefer not to judge," I said.

"Well then that's a serious problem, you should judge, or else how will you understand another person?"

"I do judge, but I prefer not to show it." Then I asked her, a bit abruptly, "Would you like to go for a drink?"

"Sure, why not? What else do we have to do on a Sunday night? But I am feeling too lazy to go to a restro-bar. Let's go back to my place."

"Not a problem," I said, and asked for the cheque. She stood up and I thought, man, she is hot, why would she ask me to come to her place? She was meeting me for the first time, after all. I got a little excited. Maybe I was about to hit jackpot today.

We reached her residence at around ten. She had a well-furnished, two-room apartment; the hall had a small fish aquarium, and next to it was a bar.

"What do you drink?" she asked, putting her handbag on the low glass table.

"Scotch, if you have some, or else anything goes for me."

"Well," she said, "even I prefer scotch."

I smiled, enjoying the turn of events.

"Let me go to the kitchen and get something to eat. Make me a drink please, and one for yourself as well," she said and smiled.

"As you say, Ma'am," I said as she left for the kitchen. While I was making the drink, my phone began to vibrate. It was Ridhima! I got nauseous. I wanted to answer her call; I wanted to know why she was calling me. I was about to answer it, when the phone stopped ringing.

I poured some Scotch for both of us, put in a couple of ice cubes, and mixed the drinks while heading towards the kitchen. Deepali had nachos in the oven. I handed her the drink and she leaned on the sink while holding the glass.

I smiled at her. She smiled back. I looked into her eyes, and said, "I'll take your leave now. It was nice seeing you today."

She had a blank expression on her face.

"It was lovely seeing you too. Hope to catch you sometime."

The phone call had changed it all for me. I knew leaving her house was all that I could do.

Walking down the stairs, I lit a cigarette. I walked towards my car, attached my cell phone to the car stereo, and tuned into the Rolling Stones song, 'You can't always get what you want!' I had it on loop and drove homewards. On the way I saw the signs on the huge blue boards:

234 kms Jaipur, Rohini 3 kms

I stopped the car in the middle of the road and took a left towards the Jaipur highway.

I started driving towards Jaipur at a constant speed of a hundred kilometres an hour. I had crossed heavy-duty loaded trucks every ten seconds for two hours. I lit the last cigarette in the pack and started searching for a place to halt. I saw a board on my left saying 'Shambu Ka Dhaba – 2kms'. I decreased the speed of the car and started driving on the left side, then parked the car in front of the dhaba and got out. There were a few plastic chairs and four wooden tables right next to the kitchen. I grabbed a chair and rested my butt, and shouted for some food, "Bhaiya, *kuchh khane ko milega?*"

A man wearing a white vest and a green shorts said, "*Aya ji. Ek* minute."

I asked him to get me some tea, and drank two glasses of water to cure my dehydration; then took out my phone and called Deepali.

"Too early to wish you good morning?" I asked.

"Yes, certainly," she said, her voice husky.

"Well, I just called to check whether you had slept or were still awake."

"I had gone to sleep until the phone vibrated."

"Fine, Deepali, have a good night."

"Yes, I will, you have a good night too," she said.

And I drank my cup of tea, asked Shambu to arrange a pack of cigarettes for my drive back home and left, listening to the Rolling Stones.

The next day, driving back home from the gym, I opened the dashboard for my phone and dialled Ridhima's number. The phone rang, and I immediately disconnected the call. Why had I called her? I used to call her after I was done at the gym on my way home, I thought. Old habits die hard, I guess.

I started questioning my thought process. I had always believed that you should have power over your thoughts and take steps in the chosen direction so as to not to lose control over life. Happiness could only be obtained if you have control over your life in all its aspects – your career, your family, societal and personal needs. And if you lose track of any one of the aspects, you would end up disturbing the appearance of all in your head.

People may come up to pat your back, trying to cheer you up, but you know it was not that simple; nobody in this world has the potential to look into a person's mentality. Maybe that's why it is said that if you can look inside your own heart, you might find all the answers you are looking for. The truth is that we are all the same – the so-called social beings, stuck in a vicious circle from which there is no possible escape.

I knew all this way too well, and I had been way too cautious too, but with time I had lost it and knew I was no longer a master of my thoughts. I was learning it the hard way, maybe the hardest way. Some people have the potential to fuck you in every possible position described in the *Kamasutra*. All I had to do now was to be flexible enough and ready for any position in which life was about to fuck me.

Flashback

20 January 2014

Ridhima and I were driving to the wedding of my friend's sister. I seemed to have lost the way.

"Ridhima, are you aware of any short cut from Sainik Farm to Chatarpur Farms?" I asked her.

"No, I am not," she said, a bit aggravated.

"Well, please turn on Google maps," I said.

She did and started giving me directions. I felt a weird sensation listening to her voice; her voice had the potential to melt me. She was a perfect combination of voice and body.

We reached a dark, steep lane. I could see a huge entrance gate, but no lights. No watchman or any other soul was around. It was a secluded farmhouse and I took the car in and then parked it. I looked around and then at Ridhima.

She gave me an innocent smile and said, "What are we doing here?"

"We are lost and we need to go back towards the city."

"How did Google map navigate us towards the wrong place?"

"Maybe we are here for a purpose. Let's try to understand it first..." I said looking at her.

"Aarush, don't talk rubbish. Let's go," she said.

I did not want to do that. "No, let's wait for five more minutes," I said.

I was wearing a grey suit, she was wearing a salwar kameez. Bright blue earrings hung from her ears and touched her soft neck. Her cheeks were flushed, and her eyes held a seductive charm. Any guy would fall for those eyes. I took her hand in my palm; she did not resist.

She said instead, "Aarush, we should leave. You behave crazily at times."

I started to rub my hand into her palms, back and forth. She did not react. I felt a little nervous. At the back of my head I knew I had entered an alien territory, and on top of it there was complete isolation, which is a very rare feat to accomplish in Delhi. I started sucking her fingers. She looked at me with a mischievous yet shy smile.

I kept on sucking on her fingers and she let out a soft moan. I started licking her neck, and she gently kept her hands on my back. I removed my coat and tried to remove her suit as well. It was a difficult tussle and she started to criticize me for doing this and said, "This is neither the time nor place for such an activity; my suit will lose its sparkle. Who is going to fix that?"

I said, "We will figure it out later."

I started working my mouth on her nipples. Her moans became louder. While I was working on those big nipples, she removed my shirt and lifted my head up and she kissed me and started licking my mouth like a lollipop.

My eyes were closed and I was enjoying the sensation. She started licking my nipples while my hands were working on hers. We were both feeling the heat of our bodies and the mist had clouded the windowpanes of the car. There was nothing visible outside, and I was experiencing an extreme sense of pleasure when she heard a noise, and said, "Do you hear footsteps... I guess somebody is walking towards the car."

I was on immediate alert and started the car. "Duck, Ridhima," I said."Wear your clothes." I started driving towards the gate with half visibility. I was half-naked as well.

I smiled a little and said, "That's the beauty of taking risks, you will remember this day for a very long time."

She said, "Shut the fuck up!"

We drove on, trying to figure out the location of the wedding.

I could not help thinking about the night when I returned early from office at four in the evening. I thought of studying, but went to bed instead and started surfing for porn on my laptop. While stroking my cock I felt a great degree of sadness. Stroking it was a tussle, but I had to do it. The sensations in my body were no longer of pleasure. I felt as if I was performing a duty, of relieving myself. Disgrace and self-pity clouded my heart and I went to sleep thinking about her and the night of pleasure.

The next morning, I woke up feeling better. I checked my phone and found two new smses – one from Vodafone and the other from Deepali.

I ignored the first one.

Deepali's read, *Hi, any plans for Saturday? I'm having a small get-together at my place. Would you care to join us?*

I was excited and replied, *As much as a get-together excites me, the thought of seeing you elevates the purpose even more.*

You're smart, she said.

Thank you for not underestimating me.

Hope to see you Saturday.

Same here.

I entered my room and started to scribble notes from my sociology book again. I was on Chapter seven, titled 'Sanksritistion and Westernization'.

After a few hours, I messaged Deepali again, for my mind was restless.

Care for a coffee today?

We decided to meet at 8:30 p.m. at Café Coffee Day. I went downstairs to have a cigarette. I asked the panwadi, but he was out of my regular brand.

My restlessness increased. I went inside the park, sat on a cold concrete bench under the shade. There were people jogging, children were playing cricket, and everybody looked as if they had a purpose to their lives. I on the other hand was sitting on this bench all by myself, with no energy to even get up and start walking towards a better future.

I started to wonder what was really going on in my life, why I was experiencing this extreme sadness and dullness. If somebody was to look at me, he would clearly make out that I was miserable and pathetic.

I just sat there wondering what the fuck I had been doing in the past two-and-a-half years. It could not be Ridhima alone who was responsible. She was the one who acted as a trigger, but there were numerous internal issues that had made me reach the point I was at. Had I really become a face in the crowd, who lived to eat, breathe and sleep?

I had left journalism for a reason, because I no longer believed in media houses. I felt they were way too commercialized and lacked the basics of news-telling. It had been two-and-a-half years since then. And I was miles away from being an author; from being someone who lived to share knowledge, someone who lived to share emotions. Somebody who had a purpose in life.

At what point did I lose it? Was it because of the idiotic job I was stuck in, or was it because of trying to get an admission into a decent college for my Master's degree which was more like a battle in India, where you fight alone with nobody on your side. I had no fucking idea where I had lost it; all I could feel was the pressure. It was as though I was inside a pressure cooker, ready to whistle out, ready to hit the world. But instead, I was a pressure cooker without a whistle; my pressure was neither seen nor heard.

My phone vibrated and I came back to my senses. I started to walk towards my car. I had to hit the gym. After all, it was the only place where I could feel alive.

At 7:30 in the evening, I returned from the gym and rushed towards the bathroom to get ready. My mother had already prepared my protein shake which I drank in a gulp.

I checked my wardrobe and realized I had no clothes of my own! I had two white shirts, and three t-shirts that I wore to the gym; the rest were clothes that Ridhima had given me. My wardrobe spoke a different story. She might have really loved me, after all. I started to hunt through the clothes, and managed to get a white shirt and a pair of jeans to wear.

At Café Coffee Day I got myself a latte, and a Chicken65 while she ordered a black coffee without sugar.

"So how did your day go?" I asked her.

She looked cool and unflustered. "Boring as usual," she said, "nothing new is coming up though there are a number of projects in the pipeline. I really want to go on a holiday, but that's impossible."

I looked at her and asked, "What exactly do you do, Deepali?"

"Well, as a marketing consultant I sit in my cabin and work on assigning and investing in new projects. I also design marketing strategies so that the company may reach new heights."

"So any progress in taking your company to new heights?"

"Well, I've sustained myself here for the last five years. That should count for something," she said.

My head started to hurt. I have never really been too fond of corporate culture.

I said, "I believe you have more in you."

She said rather seriously, "I believe so too. But tell me Aarush, what keeps you rolling?"

"Life…" I said, "life keeps me rolling."

"You have your office today?"

"Yes, I will be leaving in a while," I said.

"Are you comfortable working at nights?" she asked.

"Hell no, not at all," I responded. "To be honest, I hate my profession, but the poor man's got to eat."

"Oh, so what do you want to do?"

"I want to be a writer, Deepali, that's all I want to be."

Our cups of coffee were almost over and I had to rush to office, so we ended our rendezvous.

I decided to drop her before going to work. As we were driving, she said, "I am so glad I met you."

"So am I."

"Although we had a vulnerable first meeting, but I am glad it happened. Not the accident, but our interaction," she said and kissed my cheek before saying goodbye. What a woman she was!

As I entered Deepali's apartment on Saturday, I saw a bunch of corporate maniacs present. Middle-aged morons who were trying to impress women younger than them by exhibiting their Tommy and Armani attires, and with iPhones in their hands. Women in their mid-thirties, trying to ensure their youth was not lost and that they still had it in them, lounged around. They looked rather hot and I guessed that they knew that very well.

I went searching for Deepali, and found her in the kitchen wearing a black sleeveless gown, with little stones embedded around the neck of her gown. Her eyes seemed bigger and she looked younger to me than before. We smiled at each other. She leaned forward and gave me a little kiss on my cheek. I did the same to her. She started introducing me to her friends. I somehow felt as if she had called me to flaunt me as her 'young' friend.

Deepali introduced me to her friend Ishita, a chubby, thirty-something woman wearing a green gown and also to Akshay, a middle-aged fellow, who spoke to me as if I was a nobody while flaunting his BMW keys around. I was fine with it. After a while, Akshay took his parade somewhere else and I got busy talking to Ishita. We both held green beer half-pints in our hands and discussed astrology. She said she was a Reiki healer, and felt good when she could be of help to others, I understood, she must have gone through a lot in her life.

I asked her, "What made you choose this profession?" while my eyes wandered to her chest. She caught the glance but ignored it. She said something, but the music was too loud, so I hardly understood anything.

We went towards the dining area where we found Deepali dancing. She was making insane noises as she stumbled about. here and there. I somehow felt that the fish in the aquarium were also noticing her, thinking who would give them food tomorrow if something happened to her. Her happiness and alcohol were at the peak, and she hardly seemed to care about it.

I looked at Ishita. She looked at me and smiled. Deepali came towards me, and holding my hand, led me towards the balcony. There was no one there.

She asked for a cigarette. I gladly gave it to her. She said, "Thank you for coming."

"Pleasure is all mine," I said. "What really makes you happy, Deepali?"

She said, "I don't know, with time I guess I have lost the real meaning of happiness. It's just time, and it never stops. Everything is temporary, and I want to make the most of it."

"You never felt like getting married again?"

"I have never really understood the concept of an arranged marriage. Moreover, men tend to stay away from a widow; they don't want to marry them, or they just like to fulfill their sexual desires with them. So I don't consider it. "

I could not trust her words. I somehow felt she was trying to lure me with her words. It had been seven years since her husband's death. Nobody was that impractical in today's scenario, and she was definitely not the kind.

I said, "Open the gates to the world some day. You never know what's in store for you, till the time you search for it."

"Where do you get all these words from?"

"Certain things should be kept secret," I said flicking the ash from my cigarette.

"Let's go inside, it's my party," she said.

We went inside, and I bumped into Akshay again. He fetched me a drink and both of us sat on the sofa and drank, without talking to each other. Ishita walked up, "Let's click a picture," she said. I hated it when anybody asked me to get clicked, but I managed to smile.

It was getting late and people were leaving. I went up to Deepali to say bye to her, but she asked me not to leave, and to wait for a while. Ishita said bye to me and left. Deepali and I were alone now. She was drunk and her house was a mess. I started wondering what she wanted from me, and why she had stopped me from leaving with the others.

She asked for a cigarette, and we sat on her sofa and smoked. She looked tired, so I asked her to go to sleep.

"Yes, I should," she said.

I looked at her. She made no move to get up. "Deepali, I think I should leave," I said, really wanting to leave.

She again insisted that I wait. "You don't have a girlfriend, do you?" she asked me.

"No, I don't."

"That's why you are wasting your time with me."

"Maybe, maybe not... I am here because it feels good to be with you."

She blushed a little. I could see sleep in her eyes, so I walked her to her bed. She fell asleep in no time. I was not sure whether to stay or to leave.

I went outside, got myself a beer, sat on the sofa, and again started wondering what the fuck was going on. The smoke was inside my head, I just didn't know what to do. It felt good being there, but my heart was somewhere else. I laughed, this time a little loud. I finished my beer and went to sleep on the couch.

It was around 8:30 a.m. that Deepali woke me up with a smile on her face. "Aarush, I thought you had left," she said.

"A man never runs away from his duty," I said, rubbing the sleep from my eyes.

She gave me a bottle of water, and sat next to me on the couch. Our eyes were on the bar. The place was a complete mess. There were empty packets of chips and beer bottles all over the place.

She looked at me and I looked at her. We both knew what was about to happen next. I held her hand, and leaned towards her. She closed her eyes, and we kissed. We started running our hands over each other's bodies. Her tongue was all over my lips and I felt like a mere puppet in her hands, but then all of the sudden she stopped, and asked me to leave.

I got agitated and took no time to walk out of her apartment. I sat in my car, angry as hell. The sun was out and it was hot. I took out my sunglasses, and drove home in a fury.

❖

"Where were you?" Asked my mother as I walked in.

I said, "Office, I got late."

"Since when have you started working on Saturdays?" she asked.

"From today," I said. I got myself another bottle of water, went to my room, and dozed off.

When I woke up around three in the afternoon, I checked my phone and saw a new message from Deepali.

It was nice seeing you, Aarush.

I got more agitated. I felt like cursing the entire breed of womankind. I left the phone where it was, stepped out of my room, and asked Maa to give me something to eat.

The next night I was back at work, and when at two I was standing in the office cafeteria, smoking a cigarette, my manager came towards me, gave me my salary check, and said, "I don't think you can work in this organization anymore."

I felt like slapping him there and then, not because he asked me to leave, but because that fellow thought I was not worthy to work in the company.

But like always, I controlled my thoughts and said, "That's fine."

I left with a smile on my face. I could not figure out whether I was happy or sad. I was relieved in a way; I would not have to come and face the bunch of idiots and scammers anymore. At the same time, I was concerned about my finances. I started my car, and tuned in to Kerry Roger's, 'The Gambler' on my stereo', lit a cigarette, and left for home.

❖

The next day, I got my textbooks out and started studying, way more determined to get admission into a decent college. The only possible solution now was to study. I took a break in the afternoon and was sitting in my mother's room when I glanced at her phone. I remembered that Maa was still in touch with Ridhima, so I immediately took her mobile and went to her WhatsApp chat list. I wanted to see Ridhima. In her profile picture, she was posing in front of the banner of her radio channel, and looked okay. Why had she left me? What wrong had I committed? How could somebody do this to me? I began to wonder again and started sweating and experiencing the pain below my heart again. I decided to write an email to her:

You are a pathetic woman. I sincerely wish I could forget the three years that I have wasted with you. I never liked you. I knew you were miserable, dumb and idiotic. Don't even dare to try and get in touch with me, or try to manipulate me emotionally. I know people like you are born mediocre with no real sense or consciousness. Always selfish and pathetic, it is people like you who bring disgrace to love and relationships. I will never ever get in touch with you again, and you dare not message or contact me again.

I don't even wish you all the best,
Just go to hell!

As I entered the washroom, I had tears in my eyes. I opened the tap and started splashing water on my face as quickly as I could and then sat on the washroom floor. The tap water was still running and so was my sobbing. My t-shirt was drenched with my tears. Every part of my body was singing tunes of misery and hollowness, and I was lying on the floor, crying in disgrace. I felt like breaking the shaving mirror, but I knew that was not the solution. I had no strength left and my mind was blocked. After e-mailing her, I was way more anxious as I knew the wait for her reply would be a long one.

Later in the evening, I sat in the park on a concrete bench, just looking at my phone, hoping she would reply, hoping she would abuse me and give to me ten thousand reasons as to why she left.

The sun was sinking and I kept looking at my cell phone in vain.

Travelling to Lahaul-Spiti

$\mathcal{O}$ne-and-a-half months later, I entered the entrance hall of a government school somewhere in South Delhi. I wondered whether doing my Master's and getting admission in a reputed college was the answer to all the misery I had bestowed upon myself. My nervousness was reaching its peak and I was hoping for a favourable result. My concern was about my handwriting; it was worse than that on a doctor's prescription. As I entered the classroom, I could see some students from the Northeast, some candidates from Bihar, some from South India and several others. I sat to appear for the examination, and the invigilator gave me the test paper. The moment I had the questions, I knew I would be able to complete the test. But would it be good enough to get me a seat in JNU was something I would have to wait to discover.

As I completed my test I felt lighter under my skin, and light in my head. I had no clue how the test had gone but I told myself that I had given it my best shot. I went out, smoked a cigarette, sat in my car and played some retro tracks. I decided to drink some beer on my way home and I called Nikhil. He left his office in Malviya Nagar so that we could go back home together. When he arrived, we went in search of a bar and got ourselves some chilled beer.

The next morning I woke up with a dry mouth and bruises on my body. I could vaguely remember what had happened. I looked around and saw that I was in a very dirty, filthy room. I could smell urine and was lying on the floor, half-naked. Next to me was Nikhil, lying unconscious, but breathing. There was blood on his left leg. There were big iron bars surrounding us, and policemen in their khaki uniform walking freely outside.

I said to myself, Dammit, what have I done? I had never witnessed a prison before so it took me some time to figure out that I was in a prison cell.

I called out to a policeman, "Sir, what wrong did I commit? Why am I here?"

He said, *"Beta, iska jawaab toh court me he milega."*

"But Sir, at least tell me what wrong I have committed?"

He said, *"Chupkar gandu, pada reh vahin par!"*

I went to Nikhil and tried to wake him up, but he was unconscious and did not react. I started to panic. I had no idea where I was – Delhi, Gurgaon or Noida, and as to what crime I had committed. Maybe it was an accident? Had I been caught with a prostitute? It could also be that Ridhima was responsible for this... I might have gone to her apartment and created a scene. I had no fucking idea; my hand was paining and my head was spinning like I was on a merry-go-round.

I sat for a minute or two and then started to check my pockets. I could not find anything. My wallet was also missing. I glanced at Nikhil and saw that he was struggling to regain consciousness.

When he did, I asked him, "Are you all right?"

He slapped my face. I was rather shocked but kept my cool.

"Could you please tell me what the hell happened last night?" I asked him in an agitated tone, in between breaths.

"*Bhosdike*," he cursed, "you slapped a policeman."

I was stunned. I could not remember anything. "Dude, don't fuck with me."

Nikhil slapped me again and said, "Yes, you did that. What else could have possibly happened?"

I started to believe him. In my subconscious, I always knew one day I would end up getting into fight with a police officer. I always hated the cops in Delhi from the core of my heart. This was also one of the major reasons I wanted to pursue law, so that no law administrator could ever mess with me. I started to laugh aloud. Nikhil looked at me, his face red, and he started beating me again. "*Haramzade*, you think this is a joke?" And I kept laughing.

I said, "Nothing can possibly go wrong. All we need to do is bribe these losers a little bit and apologize to them innocently. Stop panicking."

So I pleaded to the officer to let me make a call. I called a few friends and we bribed them with ten thousand rupees; we were out in no time.

Nikhil looked at me, still angry. I knew he could not stay angry with me for a very long time. We had been friends for centuries.

We sat in the car and he told me how I had been drunk like hell and could hardly keep my eyes open. He was driving the car, when a police barrier stopped us. He was handling the situation when I got out of the car and started cursing them. When the policeman started to approach me, I slapped him as I hard as I could. The noise was so loud that the other policeman, who had been sleeping, woke up and we were brought to the Inderlok police station.

At home, my mother was just happy to have me back home. She did not ask me any questions, just held me tight and told me not to do something like this ever again.

It was at around two that night that I sat up alone in my room watching *Braveheart* when my hands went to the cellphone and I dialled Ridhima's number. First there was no answer, second call no answer, third call no answer, but she did answer the twentieth call.

"What the hell is wrong with you? Please don't disturb me," she said.

I told her, "I am not well, please help me."

"Well, if you are not well, go and see a psychiatrist."

I tried to speak, but could not. I somehow managed to say, "Why are you not helping me?"

She said, "Don't disturb me!" and disconnected the line. I kept staring at the phone for some time. Then I went to my sister, woke her up and started crying. She asked me what was wrong.

I said, "I just don't know, but something is definitely wrong with me." And I continued sobbing while she gave me a blank uncomprehending look. After the melodrama, I dozed off to sleep.

Next morning, I woke up with a headache, and nausea. I went to the kitchen and gulped a bottle of water when flashes of the past night triggered within me.

I started laughing. How could someone be so stupid, where was the self-respect? Did she really deserve that kind of power over me? I have to be stronger than all this nonsense, I said to myself, and went out to have a cigarette. While smoking, I took out my phone and called Deepali. I wanted to meet her, but she said she was only free the next day.

"Let tomorrow come," was all that I said.

The next day, I sat in the park, smoking a cigarette . It was a Monday morning, and monsoons were marching their way to Delhi. I was sitting in the hut in the middle of the park, enjoying the rain, watching dogs fighting under the tree nearby, when my phone rang. It was Ridhima! I did not respond. She called again, and I ignored the call, and she did not call after that.

The time had come to let her go. More than her, it was time to set myself free.

I called Nikhil and asked him if he would be interested in going to Lahaul-Spiti. He was game. "So you pack your bags, we will be leaving tomorrow morning," I told him.

"Will you get the tickets and make the other arrangements?" he asked.

"Yes, leave everything else to me, you make sure you are ready on time," was what I told him.

I went back home and booked two tickets for Shimla, and then two from Shimla to Rekong Peo.

The next day, we were running a little late, so we ran to the inter-state bus terminus, and breathing heavily, we managed to catch the bus.

"Thank you, Nikhil, for making this trip possible. I was so desperate to leave town," I said and then I started chanting the Hanuman Chalisa, praying to god to let this trip help end my pain and make me return a better person.

Nikhil was busy talking to his girlfriend and explaining something to her. Then he was busy talking to his second girlfriend, giving her some other kind of explanation. Soon, I dozed off to sleep. Nikhil woke me up, for the bus had stopped for a couple of minutes at Karnal. It was a trifle cold outside and we shared a cigarette.

Nikhil said, "So Aarush, when will you stop taking decisions without any plans, and keep making plans without any prior notice?"

This aggravated me. "I told you a day before we were to leave, isn't that notice enough?" I asked.

"No it isn't. You have no idea how many excuses I had to make to take leave from office…"

"I will make sure it is worth it, my friend, do not worry," I told him, not wanting his words to spoil my happiness.

"You are an asshole," said Nikhil, but he grinned.

"Who knows it better than you?" I put my hand on his shoulder and we went back inside the bus. Early in the morning, the bus dropped us at the old bus station of Shimla and we took the first bus to Rekong Peo. The bus was really small and Nikhil was fairly huge.

I looked at him, and he looked at me, "Dude, what the fuck, I told you we should hire a bike. I cannot travel in this bus," said Nikhil.

"Nikhil, if we had travelled by bike, we would have missed the ways of the locals," I said.

"Screw you and your local shit, there is no way I am travelling in this bus."

"There is no other option," I told him point blank.

The passengers were all villagers. We hardly had any place to sit. Both of us were sitting on one seat, and the journey was fourteen hours long. It had started raining and after crossing Narkanda, we witnessed the first landslide. A group of villagers got out to remove the stones on the road, and make way for the bus to cross. It was a scary sight; on the left of the road the valley was deep and the river was flowing with an aim to wash away any living or non-living object that would come in the way. Everybody got out of the bus. I was scared, and Nikhil seemed to be on the verge of experiencing his first heart attack.

There were gigantic stones on the road. The locals, singing songs of motivation in their own language, were removing the stones on the road using their bare hands. I tried to help them. After half an hour, we managed to clear the path of the landslide. I was exhausted. We were travelling on the most dangerous road in the world, and our life was in the hands of a bus driver; who looked half-drunk and half-asleep to me. In the background there were traditional Himachali songs being played, and they provided us some relief.

We got a room as soon as we reached, and left to enjoy a scenic view of Kailash Parbat. We were supposed to take a taxi towards Kalpa, but I insisted on trekking. Nikhil started recording the view, and I was enjoying the cold wind, the green fields and tall trees.

Nikhil had begun to curse me for making him trek so much. An army truck passed by and we asked for a lift. They were kind enough to allow us to hop in. I was fascinated to hear from them about the way they travelled. What sounded like an adventure to me, was nothing but routine for these army men. I had had no idea about how motivated these soldiers were.

The next day, we spent time visiting local caves in Rekong Peo, and tasting the local wine of Himachal. It tasted sweet and made me feel a little slow and nauseated. At night we had a bonfire and drank some more. We sat enjoying the tales and stories told by the locals sitting with us around the bonfire – tales of their faiths and beliefs.

One of the locals – who worked at a nearby dam, spoke English and wore Tommy Hilfiger – told me the story of their local goddess. Of how they still offer her goat's meat every six months. He believed that it was because of the goddess that their village had never witnessed a landslide.

I wish I could tell him it was not that simple, but I was glad that he had satisfied his soul based on myths associated with his village, so I preferred not to comment. Instead, I just enjoyed the story.

I opted to stay for a day or two more in Shimla. Nikhil decided to go back home, so we both parted ways the next morning. That day, I relaxed on my own, enjoying the natural environs so different from Delhi.

The following morning, a call from Deepali woke me up.

I answered her happily, "Good morning! To what do I owe the honor of receiving a call from you at this bright hour?"

"Well, I just wanted to check whether you are a morning person or a night person?"

"Well, I used to be a morning person but my night shift screwed me pretty badly, and now I am trying hard to tussle with the sunlight. How are things with you?"

"I took an off for three days, wanted a break. To lie down on my bed and do nothing."

"Well, if this is your plan, then why don't you take a bus to Shimla? I am here, and my plan is the same as yours; there's only a change in location."

"You should have asked me earlier, I would have definitely accompanied you," she said.

"So is it too late for me ask?"

"No, not really. I'll take the bus in the evening and see you tomorrow morning," she said.

"Sounds good to me," I said, grinning into my phone.

I was surprised that she was up for it. I booked her the tickets and next morning, went to pick her up from the bus stand.

As she walked towards me with a haversack on her back and a hood cap on her head, I found her extremely appealing. Her lips were pink, her cheeks rosy. She looked excited as she came towards me and hugged me.

At the hotel, she seemed a little tired from the journey. I ordered coffee and omelettes for both of us and then lit a cigarette.

"So, what's the plan?" she asked.

"I don't have one," I said.

"Then what are we going to do?"

"Have breakfast for sure. The rest we will figure out. What is the rush?" I was feeling relaxed.

"I am sure there are a bunch of places to visit."

"Yes, there are, but you said you wanted to lie around in

bed and do nothing. Now there is an added advantage, you can see mountains and hear the chirping of birds from the balcony, what else do you want?"

"I want to go out and observe nature closely, not from the balcony," she said, and got up and went to the washroom to shower.

I didn't know what was floating in her mind but I wanted to get into bed with her straight away. But that was me; so I let the thought pass and got dressed to go out. When she stepped out of the bath, her hair was wet. We had our breakfast and left to trek up the hill, wandering in the landscape, searching for something that was perhaps nowhere to be found.

Later that night, we went to a traditional rooftop bar. A candle in the centre of the table threw shadows on Deepali's face. Her voice sounded extra melodious to me as she said, "Let's get some rum."

We were two pegs down, sharing a cigarette, when I asked her, "So what made you come to Shimla on such a short notice?"

"I have wanted a vacation for a very long time, and you offered the perfect choice to me."

"But you could have gone with anybody else, why me?"

"Don't know, maybe because you were the only one available?"

"Well, I am hoping you know that it is an insult, because this means I am not on your priority list. What if I was not available, would you have accompanied anybody else?"

"My preference would be to ask you first, definitely, and if you were not available, then maybe somebody else," she said.

"Well, that's interesting, considering the fact you were the only one I asked to come spend time with me here in Shimla and asking anybody else never crossed my mind," I said.

"We do not share anything exclusive, I hope you are well aware of it."

"Somehow, I always lack awareness, and surround myself with hopes that tend to get twisted as situations arise," I said in an agitated tone.

"Then that is your mistake, do not put it on me," she said, blowing smoke into the air.

"Yaa, you are right." I was angry, really angry, and asked for the check. I paid the bill and left for the hotel, feeling stupid and ashamed.

After a couple of minutes, she entered the room and said, "Stop behaving like a kid, will you?"

"I have the right to feel as and when required, how I want to feel. Well, maybe you are right, I am behaving like a kid, and I am sorry but this is who I am, and I prefer to stay like this."

"Stop talking nonsense. Can we talk it through?"

"Only if you stop taking me for granted," I told her.

She took two steps forward and hugged me tightly. "No, it is not about taking you for granted, Aarush. There is a sense of insecurity in me that you will be gone one day and I will be left alone. It happens with me quite often, although it should not be an excuse to not let someone come close, but with time I have become this person."

I brought her a little more closer to myself and kissed her; she took no time to respond and kissed me back.

I got her out of the brown coat, and got into bed with her and started to undress her. I kissed her bare body; licked her navel and breasts. She started to moan like a tigress and I gripped her hands tightly, kissing her neck. She tried to get out of the grip, but I held her more tightly. After a while, she gave up. I took my shirt off and she started to work on my nipples. I unzipped my jeans, and without wasting any time, I grabbed her hair and got her into doggy style position. She started to moan rather loudly as I kept thrusting inside her for ten minutes. And then she rode me like an unsatisfied tigress – one who hadn't tasted blood for a long time.

In the morning, we ordered some breakfast. Deepali was smiling and I was feeling guilty, maybe because of Ridhima. I don't know, but my mood was off, and Deepali failed to notice it.

We left for Kufri and she said, "Thank you for making me feel special."

At Kufri, we had lunch. We then made a snowman and clicked some photographs. We then took the next taxi back to Shimla, went to our room and dozed off. We watched a movie, smoked cigarettes and drank some wine, got drunk and made love before going to sleep.

Ridhima Again

Random day, 2012

We were crossing the road at Nelson Mandela Marg, holding each other's hands.

"Aarush, promise me you will never leave my hand," she said.

I smiled and did not respond as we crossed the road and entered our college. Her class was on the first floor, mine was on the second, so we parted after the first lecture was over. Ridhima came out of her class and looked at me and we went towards the cafeteria. I noticed a ring on her finger, and I lifted her hand and asked her when she had got the ring.

"Two days ago," she said.

"Looks nice on you," I told her.

"I know, and it has your name engraved on the inside."

I was amazed. "Why would you do this, Ridhima? We don't need any object to prove our love for each other."

"I know, Aarush, but it makes me feel connected to you."

"I am here, sitting with you, isn't that enough?"

"Well, it is, but I just felt like getting it. It made me feel good," she said. With that she smiled, rested her head on my shoulders, and I touched her hair.

After about ten minutes, the bell rang for the second lecture and we left for our respective classes. The fact that she had worn the ring left a deep impact on me. I trusted her a little more than before, I loved her a little more than before, and I was scared a little more than I had ever been before.

Later that night, after hanging up the phone after a conversation with Ridhima that lasted around forty minutes, I pulled out my laptop and decided to write something to her. I had no clue how to match up the love she had for me, and I thought maybe writing her a letter could come close, so I started typing.

Dear Ridhima,

The world is a scary place. It has the potential to break our dreams and put them on fire and even watch us burn. So before we both get corrupt and selfish in our deeds, I would like to tell you how you made me feel today. You see, it is not about the ring, it just an ornament, but the fact that you carry my name on your finger that makes our relationship pure and pious. So I just want to say, your gesture today makes me want to be with you more than ever, makes me want to hold you and never leave your hand. I feel we both are two bodies with one soul.

I know we might be burned alive one day, but all I can say is that if you have the guts to wear me in your hands, then I certainly have the guts to keep you safe in my heart. One day when this dream ends, and you are searching for something new, remember that my heart might have turned cold and I may have turned rude and stupid, but irrespective of all the coldness, it can still keep you warm and safe for as long as you wish.

Thank you for making me feel so special always.

Love,
Aarush

Ten days after I returned from Spiti, I appeared for another entrance exam at Ambedkar College in Delhi University. After the exam, I walked out and called Deepali, and she said that a small treat was waiting for me at Café Coffee Day. I drove towards Satya Niketan and parked my car in front of the cafe. I had a smile on my face when I saw Deepali waiting for me, and I went and hugged her. She asked me if I would like to go for a movie later in the evening and I said we could.

I had started feeling comfortable around her; a sense of positivity and energy surrounded me when I looked at her. We sat and ordered coffee, and I began to discuss the question paper with her.

I leaned closer to her and said, "You look beautiful."

Deepali thanked me and smiled, and we were discussing our plan for the evening when I heard a giggle in the background. A couple of girls were laughing at the table next to ours and I recognized the giggle immediately. After all, I had heard it often enough. I looked to my right and saw Ridhima sitting at the table. Within seconds, panic mode was on a high. All the happiness was drained out of me and a sense of nervousness overcame me.

I wondered if she had noticed me sitting there. How would I react to her noticing me? My mind went blank and Deepali, noticing this, pinched me for not giving her proper attention. I returned to my senses and within that moment, I said to myself, "Fuck it, I will be as normal as I am supposed to be."

I asked Deepali if she would like another round of coffee or maybe something to eat, and she asked me what was wrong. I said that it was nothing.

Ridhima had noticed me. Both of us preferred to behave like strangers. But it was getting difficult for me to sit on the table next to her and stay calm and composed. Deepali was sure something was wrong.

She asked me, placing her coffee cup on the table, "Aarush, you must stop behaving in this abrupt fashion. It is rare for someone to have the privilege to sit and sip coffee with Deepali sitting next to him..."

"Yes, you are right, Deepali. I guess I am the privileged one."

"Yes, you are. Will you please tell me what is going on in your mind?"

"I don't know, Deepali. I want to go home, if that is fine with you."

I dropped her home. Her tone was cold as she said goodbye. I sat beneath her apartment glaring at the traffic around and then started shouting loudly inside the car and banging my head on the steering wheel. The shouts started getting louder and my head hurt. The motive was to find a channel and throw my frustration out, so I stepped out of the car and leant against the bonnet, and smoked one cigarette after another.

Ridhima's laughing face was moving all around me. How was she so happy after making me feel so pathetic? The sense of stupidity and betrayal were circling within me. Negative thoughts engulfed me.

This carried on for around half an hour, and then I decided to dial Deepali's number. She did not respond, so I climbed the stairs and rang the bell.

"Aarush! What's wrong? Either tell me right now, or please leave," she said as soon as she opened the door.

I entered her house and said, "Let me have a drink first, maybe then I will be at ease."

She said, "Who drinks this early in the afternoon?"

I said, "Whisky does not follow human time-tables."

I went towards the bar and made myself a drink and sat on the sofa.

She went inside her room and did not come out for ten minutes. After a while, she came out and sat next to me, looking at me for some sort of an explanation.

She said, "Now would you care to answer what is wrong and why your mood is swinging like the pendulum of an old wall clock?"

"My exam did not go well, so I started to panic," I said this as calmly as I could.

"Aarush, you cannot really predict the result, so better give it time. You have to stay positive."

"What if I do not clear the entrance exam? I have a seat in Pune University, but I don't want to go study in that college."

Her tone softened. "Aarush, come on, you have all the answers within you. Start searching for them."

"Ya, you are right. It is time to take some major decisions."

"All right, too much philosophy," she said.

"No philosophy is too much."

"Shut up, will you?" she said, and held me in her arms.

And for the very first time I got to know that it was not as difficult to lie to someone as I used to think. All you need is to stay confident, and divert the other person's mind from the main topic. It was more or less like a sales pitch, really.

I received a message from Ridhima that night.

You still sound the same.

None of your concern, I replied.

Hope you are doing good?

Stop messaging me. I wanted her to stop.

I want to meet you, she said.

I don't want to see you.

Please, for old time's sake, she said.

I preferred not to reply, and went out to have a cigarette. My anger had reached its peak. Look at the guts of this woman, I said to myself. How could she even think about messaging me?

Then I thought, maybe she still misses me. Maybe she is feeling guilty about what happened. But why did she want to meet me? Questions started jumping in my mind, and I had no answers.

All these answers were available with only one person, Ridhima. Somehow, every time, that woman had the potential to make my heart skip a beat, make my brain stop for a second. If this was love, then this was the most dangerous emotion any human could ever encounter, for it made you feel so powerless that you started doubting yourself.

Anyhow, keeping everything aside, while lighting another cigarette at the apartment of my rooftop, I messaged her:

Let me know when and where.

She said she would meet me at CCD at Dhaula Kuan, at 7 p.m. the next day.

I wondered whether to go meet her or not, sure that nothing good would come out of it. Then why the fuck should I see her? I asked myself and got the answer immediately. Because I wanted to!

The next evening, as I drove towards Dhaula Kaun to meet her, I had strange feelings in my head. I knew I would get angry and irritated with her. She had done nothing to make it right so far, and she really had the nerve to ask to see me again. For the first time in almost four-and-a-half years of knowing her, I realized that she does have a brain, and she is certainly using it at a right time.

She was late, as always, and I was stupid as always. I was sitting outside CCD. I lit a cigarette, and she arrived. Did she look beautiful or was she just an average looking girl? I was still in doubt, but all I knew was that I was attracted to her. From a third person's perspective, I could never comment.

She came and sat on the chair. I greeted her with a smile, and she smiled back.

I asked her, "What do want to talk about?"

She looked a little nervous. "I don't know."

"Then what do you know? You don't know why you have called me here…you don't know why we broke up?"

"Aarush, please. How have you been?"

"Struggling through the chores of my life with each passing day, like always."

"You have lost weight."

"Yes, haven't been able to work out because of the exams. I will start hitting the gym soon. What about your job, did you get into the radio channel?"

"No, they had no vacancy."

"You always knew that, then why were you wasting your time?"

"I have learned a lot in the process. It has made me a better person."

"C'mon, you are still miles away from what you want to do."

"It was an interesting chapter of my life."

"But does it fit in your story? If it is going to get edited, than what is the point?"

She drew back a bit. "You have again started to grill me."

"I am just throwing some light at you."

"Why do you do this to me?" She made a face.

"Do what?"

"Make me feel bad about myself."

"That is not my intention," I told her. "Staying away from your goal will not bring any good in your life; time is running out and really fast."

"Aarush, I am sorry for whatever happened."

"Your sorry is of no use, for the damage has been done."

"I know what you must have gone through," she said.

"No, you don't," I said. I stubbed my cigarette hard into the ashtray and gave her a direct look. How could she know?

"How can I fix this?" she asked me then.

"Fix what?"

"Fix us?"

I stopped for a second, my anger melting a little bit, but I still felt stupid. "I don't know, Ridhima. I don't think I can trust you. You have to work really hard to make it work."

"Don't you think I have given enough to this relationship?"

"Well, you have not done any favour to me."

"But I am not the same person anymore," she said, looking at me.

"Ridhima, you think there is seriously some point talking about all this now?"

"Tell me how I can make it better?"

"You cannot. And that is the problem. I need to learn how to deal with it."

"Well, have you been able to so far?"

"No, it has not been easy for me, but one thing is certain – you cannot change it now."

"Aarush, I know it is difficult, but you know me way too well...you know how I act sometimes. I don't know what I am up to at times, I am sorry. Please be with me. I want to be a better person."

I looked into her eyes and melted a little bit more. "Ridhima, after all this time, what can I do?"

"Aarush, I think I still feel for you."

"Feel what?"

"You know what..."

"Then why did you leave in the first place? Without giving any explanation, without telling me what wrong I committed, you just ran away."

"That is not true, Aarush. I told you I was not able to feel anything, my emotions were dead."

"Well, that did not mean that you needed to break up with me. As I told you, sometimes it takes longer for relationships to work. Even my life was and is not going right, but I never blamed you for anything, did I?"

I noticed my voice was getting louder, and I was sitting in an open cafeteria. I guess people were noticing us. I asked Ridhima, "Don't you think it's better that we sit inside the car?"

So we left for my car, where we sat and sat and did not talk for a couple of minutes. Then I started the car and drove towards my flat at Dwarka.

The room was a mess, and we spent ten minutes cleaning it, like old times. Then we lay on the bed, not talking to each other for the next ten minutes.

Eventually, she broke the silence, saying, "Aarush, why did this happen?"

I said, "I don't know."

"Was it my fault?"

I said, "I don't know."

"Then what do you know?" she asked me.

"That we both are back again, sitting next to each other. But is this really supposed to happen, I am no longer sure."

"Nor am I."

"Do you still love me?" I asked her.

She said, "I don't know."

"Do you want to be with me?" I asked her.

She said, "I don't know."

"Please give me an answer. One fine morning you decided that this relationship has ended, and I had to learn to live with it. It was your decision."

"Do you think we should try to work it out?"

"Well, it is not going to be easy. It's a challenge. You better ask yourself first rather than ask me."

"But you have always been the one taking my decisions when I have been confused," she said. She was putting the ball in my court.

"Times have changed, Ridhima, and it is better that you accept it."

"Of course I have accepted it. What makes you believe I haven't?" She moved slightly away from me, which I didn't mind.

I asked her, "Well then why are you asking me to take this decision for you?"

"Hmm, I want to take a nap," she said and rested her head on my chest. I somehow liked it. In an instant, she was asleep.

I smoked a cigarette or two, wondering what was happening, and then I slept as well.

I woke up after about forty-five minutes, with a smile on my face. Ridhima was asleep next to me. I swear to god I could have easily spent my life looking at her. After all, what else did I need in this world; the love of my life was right next to me.

She woke up and I kissed her forehead. She had a smile on her face.

It was ten and she had to leave. On our way back to her house, she rested her hand on my thigh. "Aarush, I am scared. There are a lot of things that you don't know about me."

"Well, the same is with me. You don't know stuff about me. But time will heal everything, Ridhima."

"But Aarush..." she protested.

I cut her short. "Ridhima, take your time, don't rush into anything. Let's start slowly and see how things resolve."

That sounded like a good idea to her.

We had reached her house and she gave a little peck on my cheek and said bye.

I took her hands in mine and said to her, "Everything will be fine, if we want this to work out. It is we and nobody else who can make it work. But promise me one thing. Whatever decision you take now, you will not back out from it in the future."

After five minutes of my drive back home, I began feeling I had been used. What was Ridhima up to? She was definitely not the woman I once loved; she was some weird troubled woman who did not know what she wanted from life, and she certainly had the potential to devastate me and break me into tiny little pieces. I wondered what I should do.

I took out a cigarette and searched for a lighter. "It's a trap for sure, don't screw yourself, Aarush Mehta. Please don't do that..." the voice in my head kept saying this to me. I had no answer to any damn question. I entered my apartment gate, parked my car, and marched home.

The next morning, I started dialling the numbers of the consultants around Delhi, searching for a position in any BPO technical support department. Although I hated to be a part of this technical support scam, it was the only sector that allowed me to study and earn my livelihood together, so my options were limited and time was running out for me.

I dialled the first consultant, and he said to give him a call after a day or two. I dialled the second consultant and he asked me to come right away to his office in Malviya Nagar. Without wasting much time, I quickly changed my clothes and drove towards his office.

As I opened the office door and took three steps forward, I saw a small reception table and a not-very-presentable guy sitting on a plastic chair in front of a computer, speaking in broken English.

"Hi, I am here to speak to Mister Suresh," I said.

"He is in a client meeting. Which company have you enrolled for?"

" I am here to speak to him first and then take a call."

"Well, have a seat." The receptionist was talking to me as if Suresh was Mukesh Ambani and I was his sweeper, but I preferred to maintain my calm and silently sat on the sofa with other miserable looking guys waiting for Suresh.

Suresh arrived after fifteen minutes, wearing black trousers and a blue shirt, drenched in sweat, which made his brown neck look black. Other miserable looking masters of broken English ran towards him and Suresh acted as if he was the chosen warrior sent by the king to relieve these guys from misery and pain.

My turn came and I went inside the cabin which was the size of a cyber café cabin back in the nineties. I greeted him in a polite manner.

"Hello Aarush, please have a seat. So do you have any prior experience in technical support department?" Suresh asked me.

"Yes, I do, but unfortunately I have no documents," I said.

He told me that would not be much of a problem. They could forge the documents, and asked if I would be interested to work for a very big company in Gurgaon; they had an instant requirement. Of course I was, and so Suresh said he would arrange an immediate telephonic interview. After ten minutes, Suresh called me back in his cabin and handed me his cell phone. He asked me to speak to the HR of the company in question. I gladly took the phone and started to utter what seemed like gibberish to me, but I guess in the BPO industry you master the art of dishonesty.

They offered me thirty-five thousand rupees in hand, with cab allowance and two weekly offs, which sounded a fair deal and I accepted it readily.

Later that night I was watching *Californication* on my laptop, when Ridhima called. I was unsure whether to answer or not, and I finally decided not to answer. After half an hour, I received one more call which I answered. Ridhima said she was waiting for me below my apartment. I went downstairs and found her standing right next to my car. I was a little concerned seeing her there at such an odd hour. Luckily, I had my car keys with me, so we sat inside the car, after I had made sure that no one in the neighbourhood was looking at us. I did not want tongues wagging unnecessarily.

"What are you doing here?" I asked her.

"I wanted to see you," she said.

"Why?"

"Because I was missing you."

"You said you do not love me anymore." I was just trying to clear my mind and understand what she was up to.

"I was angry, and foolish and stupid."

"How come you are sure now?"

"Please Aarush, I am sorry for whatever happened."

I caught hold of her hand, held it tight in a vice-like grip and asked her, "Can you give six months of my life back?"

She struggled to be free. I let her go. "Aarush, even I have suffered during these six months; you were not alone in this."

"Then why did you do this? You were the one who said, 'Please I am sorry, I do not love you anymore'. And I was the one going crazy, manic and depressed. I was the one who was crying in the middle of the road, and you were least bothered about it. I was the one who was standing under your balcony waiting for you, or maybe a glimpse of you, and all you did was make me feel like an idiot, make me feel like a loser! You have been making a mockery of me and after all this, you still expect me to act as if everything is normal? Well, I am sorry Ridhima, the feeling of betrayal does not go away so easily.

"You need to go home now, the ship has sailed, and while on your way back, make sure you remember how you have made me feel...that will give you an answer to the question – do you even deserve what you are asking for or not?"

"Aarush, you know me too well. You know I am stupid, and can act weird and crazy at times." She made a puppy face while saying that, like she used to every time we had a fight and it was her doing.

"Your karma is not in my control. I can only guide you, not sit inside your head," I told her.

"But what will I do without you?" She was pleading with me now.

"Whatever you have been doing for the past six months: socializing, drugs, drama, chaos, Instagram, WhatsApp, snap chat, Facebook and everything else... You have taken the path of misery for yourself. I really hope that you come out of it!"

"But I need you, Aarush…"

"I don't want to be with you. Please go home now, it's getting late."

"Aarush, I am sorry," she said, but she had stepped out of the car.

I said, "We will talk tomorrow. You should be heading home now." I watched her disappearing as she walked away from me.

It was difficult for me to return home and sleep now, for my head was on the verge of an explosion. I needed some fresh air, so I drove out to have chai and cigarette.

Losing It

Two weeks later, one morning I woke up with a headache. I went to the washroom and vomited, washed my face maybe twice or thrice. The headache had overtaken my body and I could hardly walk, so I went to bed instead.

My phone rang. "I need an explanation for your leave from office yesterday," a voice said.

"Down with fever and bad cold, sir. Sorry, could not make it, but I will bring my medical certificate along..."

"You better do," said the voice, and hung up. I opened the notifications on my phone. There were five missed calls from Nikhil, five from Ridhima and seven from Deepali.

I tried to remember the previous night's events when a vague memory hit me. I could remember parts where I had a baseball bat in my hand and was running in the middle of the road, chasing a car. I got up and took a Disprin.

My mother started to shout and began asking questions one after another. I shouted right back, "Not right now, I am sleeping."

I made the first call to Nikhil. He said, "*Bhenchod, tu pagal hai kya?* Go and see a psychiatrist..."

"Nikhil, can you please listen... what did I do now?" I asked, surprised at his response to my call.

"Well, you are the one who needs to answer. What were you doing in Vikas Puri at three o'clock in the morning?"

I replied, "Dude, seriously? I do not remember anything… and how do *you* know I was in Vikas Puri at three?"

"Well, you called me twice and said, 'Nikhil please find me. I think I am about to die. I need your help.' I asked where you were and you said you were somewhere on a road in Vikas Puri and when I arrived, you were lying unconscious on the car roof. So I had to pick you up and get you inside the car. You were unconscious, and smelled like a pond with rotten fish!"

"Nikhil, I swear the only moment I can recall is running with a baseball bat in the middle of the road and chasing a car."

"Aarush, please don't do this to yourself. Sleeping on the top of the car bonnet… what is wrong with you, man. I am really concerned about you."

"I know you are, and I am sorry for yesterday's incident. Give me some time…I will get back to you."

I called Deepali after that. She sounded concerned and asked whether my head was still paining. I told her I had a headache. Then she said, "Please do not behave in this manner ever again. You scared the hell out of me. I was clueless as to what was happening. You had so much anger inside you. Do you have a split personality disorder? You look happy most of the time and then all of a sudden you become a man with a vengeance."

I ignored her statement and asked her, "Can you please tell me what happened last night. I hardly remember anything."

She started to talk.

"You entered my house around 10.30 p.m., drunk. We sat and had a couple of more drinks for an hour or so and you got up to use the washroom and ended up puking all over the place, so I asked you to stay for the night. You refused, but I somehow managed to make you sleep for an hour or so.

"Then you left, and I received a call from you around three and you said, 'Deepali, please tell me I have been nice to you, that I am a good person…' I asked you where you were and you said that you were going to die, you could see the end approaching. I again asked you about your whereabouts and you thanked me for being a part of your life. Then you told me you were in the middle of nowhere. I heard some cursing in the background and people shouting your name and then you hung up and did not answer the phone after that."

"Wooofff… well thank you for this information and I apologize for acting like a complete psychopath."

"Aarush, who are you? Your actions amaze me every single time."

"We will discuss this someday," I said.

"Which day will that be?"

I said, "Well, it will be a full moon with the sun shining above it, bye."

The time had arrived to make the most dangerous call – the one to Ridhima. I heard her crying loudly on the other end. She said, "Aarush, please forgive me for whatever happened yesterday. I am a stupid woman dealing with a lot of stupid stuff."

"Ridhima, please stop crying, you know I am fine. So please relax and have a glass of water."

"I am fine, Aarush. I had no clue that those people would attack you. They do not behave like this generally…"

My brain started to work a little bit and images of a baseball bat entered my mind.

She continued, "It all happened because of me. I do not deserve you, Aarush."

"Who were they Ridhima? Why did they attack me?"

"Just a couple of friends," she said. "I am sorry, Aarush."

"But, why would they attack me?"

"Aarush, you were drunk and were creating a scene on the road. So I told my friends that you are my ex-boyfriend, but they all lost it the moment you pushed me right there and then and started shouting on the top of your voice. Prityush came and slapped you, followed by Sumit, and you started cursing them. Things were getting intense and you went towards your car and took the baseball bat out and started beating them up. I tried to stop all of you, but could not. Then you climbed on to the bonnet of the car and broke the windshield into pieces. I got them into the car and we all drove off as you started to chase the car..."

I asked her, "Did anybody see all this happening?"

"Well, yes, the watchman, so when I came back, I bribed him. He will keep his mouth shut now."

"How are your friends now, Ridhima?"

"Well, they are all fine. They want me to stay away from you. And I have to have them stay the fuck away from you as well, or else I may kill them all..."

Was she saying she was trying to protect me? "Thank you, Ridhima."

And without hearing her reply. I hung up.

The first thing I saw in my room was my desk, filled with books and my study lamp. I stamped my leg hard on it and some books fell onto the floor. I looked left and right, and saw the small temple in my room. I got up and threw it brutally on the floor and crunched it with my feet, and then I picked it up and threw it towards the tube light. My father suddenly came from behind me and grabbed me tightly from the back. I pushed my elbow into his face, and he went two steps backwards. Then I stopped.

My father looked at me with amazement, and said, "Aarush, you are not a civilized boy; you should not be allowed to live in a civilized place."

I said, "I am sorry, so sorry."

"Aarush Mehta, I feel sorry for you. Just look at yourself. I used to think my son is very smart, but you have broken my faith in you. I am sure something terrible must have happened in your life, but disturbing the balance of your family is going to make it worse. I thought you knew that. I guess I was wrong. Thank you for breaking the illusion."

He had let go of me, and he turned on his heel and left.

I sat on the chair. My mother came and gave me a glass of water. She said, "Aarush, it is time to fix yourself. Enough is enough."

I said, "I know, Maa. I am not this guy. I feel trapped and so powerless. I have never felt this way. I am not responsible for my actions. How do I fix myself?"

She said, "You and only you can help yourself and no one else can do it." She asked me to drink the water and go get some fresh air.

God dammit, how was I to deal with this nonsense? Ridhima had made me go crazy. I may have to go to a mental hospital because of her. Who could I hold responsible for my condition but her?

I called Nikhil and asked him to see me. There was some shit we needed to discuss.

We were standing in my balcony and I said, "Nikhil, I am fucked up, dude. What should I do?"

"Aarush, it time that you open yourself up. Move out of this city."

I was silent. I had always wanted to go to Mumbai, but never had the confidence to shift.

Nikhil spoke again, "Aarush, you are wasting your potential here. I used to look up to you, you have been my source of confidence and motivation, and today you are calling me and asking me what you should do?"

I said, "Yeah, you are right. I need to take some really tough steps in my life."

Two weeks later, the results were out, and I had not got into Delhi University or JNU.

What should I do now? I asked myself, as I waited for my office cab to arrive. I thought it was time to move out of the city; it was time to start afresh. It was time to move to Mumbai. But I hardly had any contacts in Mumbai. What would I do there? And how would I convince my parents?

The cab was at the Gurgaon toll plaza, and I looked at the security guard standing at the door. I asked the girl and the boy sitting next to me in the cab, "How much do you think this ticket collector earns in a month?"

The boy said, "Twenty-two thousand rupees per month".

Man, that was a lot of money, I thought. I could easily find a job like that. I could be a watchman, or a newspaper vendor.

I decided then that I was moving to Mumbai.

Mumbai

The next morning, I said to my mother, "I have a job offer from Mumbai, I am leaving in a week."

My mother laughed at me, saying they would think about it. I told her I had already thought about it and planned to leave in a week's time. Her looks told me that she was not taking me seriously.

Later in the evening, I went hesitantly to my father.

I said, "Dad, I have an offer from Mumbai, a company is offering me a job as a production assistant."

And kaboom! The volcano erupted, "You have never been out of this house. You think you have the guts to live alone. It is not that simple, son."

"Dad, I have to go out, things are not right for me in Delhi. It's is time for me to move out…"

"I am not in favour of this decision, but it is your call," he said.

It was clear from their words that they were not taking me seriously. Their attitude made me even more determined. I had no job, but I knew getting out of this whirlpool would be the best for me.

The next day, I bought a train ticket and I returned home and left it on the dining table so that everybody could have a nice look at it and accept my action.

That night I was successful in convincing everyone that I was leaving and that this was the right step for me. When I came downstairs, I did start to wonder how I would manage without a job in a new city, but my heart told me something would work out.

Deepali escorted me to the railway station. I was concerned about her. I did not want her to be alone again. I asked her to visit me in Mumbai.

She said, "Very soon, my love...really, really soon."

I hugged her goodbye, and then stepped into my coach. There was an old man sitting in front of me; he smelled awful. Another fellow sitting next to me was chewing pan. I looked around this general coach of chaos and discomfort and said to myself, "Aarush, your life will never be the same; you will never be the same. Embrace it, accept it and live with it."

I was happy in a very nervous way, like a warrior preparing for combat. The train started and I chanted the Hanuman Chalisa three times, rested my ass on the top sleeper and dozed off to sleep.

I reached Mumbai at four in the morning, and took an auto to 7, Bungalow Road where my friend Jacob lived. I had three bags with me, and when I reached Jacob's home, I called him up, asking him to come downstairs. We sat there and talked for ten minutes, going down the memory lane, remembering and recounting incidents from our college days together. Then I asked Jacob if I could stay with him for a while. Jacob told me that I could not stay there, since he was sharing the space with two other guys, but I could spend the night.

I woke around eleven o'clock in the morning. There were two guys sitting on the folding bed not talking to each other, busy on their phones. I was lying on the sofa, feeling a little embarrassed as Jacob was nowhere around. However, I got up and said hello to both of them.

Jacob soon arrived. I had a bath and dressed and went down with him to a nearby restaurant to have breakfast. I told him I had no plans and he suggested that I go to town where there would be many places to visit. But I told him I wished to go to Lonavala instead, so he dropped me at the bus station after breakfast.

On the bus to Lonavala, I plugged in my headphones and tried to contemplate my next move. For three hours, my mind wandered from left to right: from the people and the culture of Mahrashtra, to the scenic view outside. I was feeling free. I had a new set of troubles in my life, but all the old troubles were out in the air.

On reaching Lonavala, my first target was to find a cheap…no, the cheapest hotel. It took two hours, but I managed to get a room for five hundred rupees. I asked the receptionist if he could get me some beer from the nearest wine shop, and after fifteen minutes he got me eight pints of beer and smiled at me and said, "Sir, you have a good night."

I woke up in the morning and hydrated my body with a bottle of water. Sleeping naked was an experience in itself. You do not feel shame and start to love you body. I got out of the blanket and started to pose in front if the mirror and checked my biceps. I did have a decent physique, better than many, and cigarettes would surely ruin it one day, I said to myself as I went towards the washroom to have a bath.

I checked the internet and found the numbers of a couple of brokers in Mumbai, who could help me find a room in Versova, Mumbai. In the middle of the afternoon, I called a few of them and arranged meetings for the next day, then packed a small bag and a water bottle and some biscuits, and started taking a walk to the sunset point in Amby Valley, Lonavala.

It was around five in the evening, and the brightness of the sun had started to fade. A dog accompanied me on the short journey as I managed to lure him with some biscuits. When I reached the top of the hill, I found a comfortable spot and sat down. The dog took the spot next to me. I closed my eyes and tried to keep my mind vacant.

After a while, images of familiar faces started to float in my mind – from Ridhima to Deepali to my mother, father and Nikhil. I could see them all smiling; some even laughing. I thought they would all forget me one day. We human beings have a tendency to move on in search of happiness and are familiar with the mechanism of how to achieve it through our little magic tricks. I wondered when I would learn all these magic tricks, when my laugh would not be out of self-pity and misery. When would I laugh in happiness? Another voice in my head said, "Aarush, not anytime soon."

The slanting rays of sun made my eyes feel a little warm and I opened them. The sun seemed to be talking to me now.

The sun said to me, "I am going for the day and the moon will come up and take my spot at the top of the sky, but do not forgot that the light that makes the moon shine comes from my heat, and tomorrow morning the moon will be gone and I will be back again with much more brightness and spark.

"During this process, I do not waste my time. But you better ask yourself what have you been up to since the last six months? How much more time are you planning to waste in trying to make yourself feel happy and alive? Look around, nobody really cares about you; it is your responsibility to fix yourself. I get back in every twelve hours, and shine for the rest of the day, but you have been sleeping the past six months – just a walking-dead. Just imagine the possibilities: you could have completed the first draft of the novel you always wanted to write, you could have learned horse riding or learned paragliding or anything else. Unfortunately, this time will never come back, Aarush Mehta, it's time to get up and face the world, and face it hard indeed."

I was feeling really light at that moment. My entire life was moving in front of me as if the sun was a theatre hall and the cigarettes and water bottle were my popcorn and coke. I saw myself as a kid playing cricket, crossing the entire length of the swimming pool in one breath, playing chess with my father and the CBSE Board exams, my first girlfriend, my first salary check, and the NEWS7 office. These images were all in front of me and I managed to smile. The sun was going down, getting lost in those hills and I was gaining whatever little strength from the light.

I had to explore my true potential, my inner self. I was yet to set myself free.

❖

The next morning, I got up and looked around. I somehow managed the strength to get up and grab the bottle of water lying on the floor. I then got dressed, packed my bag, left the hotel, and took the next bus to Mumbai. I went straight to the broker and then with him to check out the PG nearby. The kind of budget I had, I was not going to get anything fancy. The rooms were small and ugly, their aura filled with struggle and disappointments. I was prepared for it. So I decided on the second room I saw. It would not do much for me to look further.

I said, "How much is the rent for this room?" "Sir, ten thousand rupees per month, two months' advance rent and ten thousand security."

I said my budget was not more than eight thousand. He said that was not possible. The owner would not permit it. So I asked to be taken to the owner and negotiated with him and settled for eight-and-a-half. I gave him the token money.

I got my luggage from Jacob's house, took a rickshaw and left for my new home. It had a small bed on one side, and a kitchen adjacent to it. I had a smile on my face for I knew what I had got myself into and I was fucking prepared for it. I took my laptop out and started to search for jobs, and upload my resume. I was alone, all alone. I went the nearby wine shop and treated myself to a quarter of rum, came back and dozed off to sleep.

And finally I did get a job; not one of my dreams, but one nevertheless.

The Job

$\mathcal{A}$s I reached my office, XYZ Productions Limited, all I could see were smiling faces discussing what for me was boring and dull. I greeted everyone and sat on my seat. I switched on my computer and started working on the itinerary for a shoot in Jaisalmer. The logistics and transportation and hospitality cost as per Excel was fifty lakh rupees estimated, and I was supposed to cut it down to forty lakh rupees, without compromising on the quality of location or equipment. So the only scope I had to bring costs down was through the hotels and transport.

I went down for a smoke, frustrated, when I bumped into Vice President, Production and I started discussing the odds with him. He was a Hindi speaking drunkard who enjoyed sitting on a chair worth one lakh rupees. His dress was ordinary and his conversation was insipid, but I was counting on his experiences in life.

He told me, "You are in the service industry. You should divert your energy towards cutting the cost to thirty-five lakh rupees so that your manager relies upon you more. It is not easy, but then if it was that simple, you would not have been in this office."

He left me and I looked around, contemplating the infrastructure of this office. There were five floors and a team of roughly hundred people. It was an opaque glass building right next to Barista and ICICI Bank, at the prime location of Lokhandwala. The building would certainly be worth fifty crores and the owner of the company was yet another miserable fellow. If he could make an office here in Mumbai then I could probably be the next Prime Minister of India! I can get it down to thirty-five lakhs without any problem, I thought to myself, and left to work on my Excel sheet.

In the evening, I decided to go to the Janta Bar with my colleagues. It was a shady bar in Bandra Pali Hill, and people called it a pre-drinking bar for various reasons. The bar was shady, but the women were hot.

My colleagues were drinking and talking of how a reality show is made and the politics of the set; I was rather bored. Even after two months in Mumbai, I was still not used to the life that these guys enjoyed. I would rather have talked about tribes in Andaman than discuss which model had hooked up with which director. I was just pretending to listen, all the while trying to drink my beer in peace. Roger, one of my fellow colleagues, asked me, "So how is Mumbai treating you, Aarush?"

"The journey has been interesting so far, although I am not certain how excited and happy I am here," I said.

He said, "Give it time, you are going to fall in love with Mumbai."

I laughed aloud, "Instead, Mumbai is going to fall in love with me," and gulped my beer in one go, filled my glass and emptied it again in six seconds.

They looked at me in amazement. Roger said, "Are you in any sort of rush? Aren't we supposed to enjoy our drinks?"

I asked him, "What are the parameters of enjoyment for you?"

Roger said, "Well, certainly, talking about how I enjoy myself is not one of them."

I said, "Well, then you have no right to ask me how I enjoy my drink."

"You are weird. What are you doing in Mumbai? This is not a place for you, and this industry is certainly not, for sure."

I asked him, "How are you so sure about this?"

"Looking at your face makes me feel sure," he said.

"Roger, shut up and drink. Let's not waste our time thinking what I am supposed to do."

I did not want him to spoil my evening for me.

"Fuck off, dude! Even I am not interested in wasting my time. All I am planning to do is get one hot piece of booty to my apartment tonight," Roger said.

"Well then, you should not be here sitting with me, go and set yourself free." I poured myself another beer.

It was midnight when I came out of Janta Bar and called Deepali. There was no response. So I stopped calling and diverted my attention to my colleague who was standing in the corner talking on the phone. The road was empty, and there were hardly any people outside. I took a step forward to talk to her, and she hung up.

I said, "So Suchita, you haven't taken me to Hard Rock bar yet..."

"Well, you never gave me an opportunity."

"When are you planning to go?"

"This Saturday," she said. "Can I ask you something?"

I nodded and lit a cigarette.

She said, "You are not happy in Mumbai, right? What is it that you are looking for?"

I was drunk and these personal questions from everyone were annoying me.

"I am as happy as I am supposed to be, and I am as sad as I want to be," I told her.

"You and your lyrics, you never give a straight answer."

"Ask me a straight question and you will get a direct answer," I said.

"You make it difficult for people to communicate with you."

"I want them to concentrate on their lives and leave me alone."

The entourage came out then, drunk and happy, and our personal talk got lost somewhere between the general conversation of how the production manger of our daily soap, 'Kahani Humari Tumhari' looted the company fund. And we all left high and happy.

Next morning, I received a missed call from Deepali, but I didn't t feel like talking to her. I left for office, a place where I would spend the rest of my day dealing with models, the TRP of our daily soaps and what not.

After reaching office, I realized that the director had called to fix the schedule. When I entered his cabin, he was preparing his pipe.

He asked me to sit and said, "Would you like to share the pipe with me?"

"No thanks. I prefer to stick to my smoke sticks. This is too fancy for me," I said.

"What you call fancy, I call different."

"Whatever satisfies you." I wasn't in the mood to argue.

"So, when am I leaving for the recci? And have we been able to get the permission for the two-day shoot inside the fort?"

"Yes, we have. You leave on the second of next month, come back on the fourth morning."

"Sounds fair to me, and who else is accompanying me?" I asked.

"One Senior AD will be there with you."

"Okay, I want the art director too. I need to explain to him the detailing of props..." I said and he nodded.

"And when are we hitting the floor?" he asked me.

"Sixth morning."

He was not happy. "This gives me only one day to rehearse with the team."

The permission is for the seventh and eighth, so yes, that is the only day you get," I said.

"I cannot do it in a day."

"I am sorry but they are not willing to provide any other days. They have a local festival starting on the tenth, so those were the only available dates..."

"What nonsense, Aarush! I need at least two days."

"That is not possible for me."

"I need to talk to the production; you are not solving my problem. I need two days to understand the location, fix my cameras, put shots on paper, get my lighting right. It is a lot of work and a little bit of understanding is required from you. Or else I have to talk to the production head if you cannot get me two days."

I was firm. "That is your call. I did whatever best was possible. A person like you should be able to get all this done in a day."

"I can, but that does not mean I want to," he said. He tapped his pipe on the ashtray.

"Then you can talk to anybody you want," I said, not bothered really.

"Fine, you may leave. You have messed up with my head," he told me.

I came out irritated. He was an idiot and nothing more than that for me. It was not like I could not get him permission for another day, but I just did not want to.

I wanted him to suffer, to create a scene, so that people knew that the worth of this guy was nothing.

In the afternoon, my immediate boss asked me to come to his cabin. I knew what it was about.

"What can we do to fix the problem? There has to be some way...you have to fulfil the needs of the director."

"Sir, the only solution is that the crew leaves one day prior, and gets to stay in Jaisalmer. They do not come back on the fourth."

"But I have to attend the wedding of a close friend," said the director, sitting there.

I did not look at him. "Sir, that is the only option I can provide. So, you know, you need to take a call."

He said fine, and left the room scratching his bald head.

My boss looked at me and said, "Aarush, I hope you know what you are doing."

"Yes, sir. I know what I am doing," I said.

"All right, you may leave."

I returned to my desk, and Suchita came running towards me, saying, "Let's go down for a smoke." She asked me what happened inside and I told her.

"The director looked puzzled for sure," she said. "He is the director of a prime time show; the stakes will be high. He is not going to let it go easily."

"Hardly matters to me. I can take his bullshit and give it right back on his face."

"But you could have at least tried to understand his situation. Poor fellow has a habit of shooting on the set. Shooting on a live location might be difficult for him…"

"Yes, it is difficult, but then he was the one who said with all the enthusiasm that they will shoot in Jaisalmer. He should have thought about it then, right?"

She changed the subject. "Are we going to Hard Rock tonight?"

"I do not have enough cash to go to Hard Rock Café," I said.

"I will ask the others too…we can share the bill. Does that sound like a plan?"

"Well, it certainly does to me, but Saturday is always crowded. There is no place in Hard Rock on Saturdays."

"Well, they play pop rock so it is bound to be crowded. Who listens to Boney M in this day and age?" she laughed.

"Well I do, for sure, and today so will you," I shot back at her as we got back to our respective desks.

In the evening, I was on my way back to my room when Deepali called.

"I have news," she said.

"When did you turn into a reporter?" I joked.

"Shut up! I will be in Mumbai in two hours!"

"That is certainly news! You have work?"

"I have a meeting day after tomorrow. I have a room in Lalit hotel. Will you came to pick me from the airport?"

"Not sure whether I can make it, Deepali. I have other plans for the day."

"Are they more important than me?"

"No, they are not, but do you want me to ditch others? I was the one who initiated the plan."

"I don't know anything, I will see you at the airport at ten."

She hung up.

I called Suchita and told her that I had a friend visiting, so would be able to join them only later.

I was standing at the Chhatrapati Shivaji Airport arrival gate, waiting for Deepali. She arrived wearing her formal attire and I felt as if I was there to pick up a client.

As she got into the car she told me that she wanted to go have coffee somewhere, but I told her that I had to join my friends sometime later.

"Let them wait, we are going to my room at the Lalit then," she said. "By the way, you look pathetic."

I told her to mind her language.

She was quiet for a minute or two. "I did not mean it the way it came out. I meant you have to start taking care of yourself."

"I know what you meant and do not intend to give any answer to you."

"Why do you always fight with me?"

"That's not my intention. I am sorry." I smiled at her and she smiled back.

At the hotel lobby, she met a colleague. She started talking to him, and started talking updates for her meeting, completely ignoring my presence. She did not even bother to introduce me.

As we entered the room, I lit a cigarette and started looking for an ashtray, and she called room service for a bottle of wine, saying, "Aarush, can you take me to Leopold Café tomorrow?"

I wanted to play difficult. "Maybe, maybe not, let tomorrow decide," I said.

She played jazz in the background, and we both sat down, sipping the wine.

She said, "Aarush, I am planning to adopt a child."

That surprised me. "But you do not have anybody to take care of the child."

"I am planning to quit my job. I have two properties in Delhi. I can manage for some time with the rent."

"You are at the peak of you career! Do you really want to give it all up?"

"Yes, I really want to. I am not getting any younger, Aarush. I want a family now. I am tired of being alone. What will I do with all the money?"

I had no answer to her question. She was right in a way. What has anybody achieved in this world with money?

"I need someone, Aarush. I want to have a baby," she said, putting her wine glass on the glass-topped table.

"Are you sure it is not out of loneliness?" I asked her.

"I don't know. My head is in turmoil these days."

I had nothing to say. I had become so self-centered dealing with my miseries that I had forgotten that there were others like me too, dealing with similar shit.

I grabbed her hand and brought her close to me. She leaned on my chest and closed her eyes. The sadness in her heart was visible on her face. The expensive room in the Lalit was of no good to her, poor woman. I started to stroke her hair, and she dozed off to sleep on the chair.

I reduced the volume of the music, finished my wine, and left her a note.

"Deepali, I am always here for you. You are not alone. We are alone together. Have a good morning."

The next morning I woke up with this message, *Aarush, you surely have some healing qualities, for you bring positivity in me, good morning!*

I went near the mirror and damn, I looked horrifying; a meth addict or maybe an alcoholic for sure. Mumbai had eaten all my meat. Then I started looking around my room. It was a mess.

"It's going be an ugly day," I said to myself thinking of the tasks ahead.

In the evening I met Deepali and we left for Leopold Café. It was crowded inside and they gave us a table after twenty minutes of waiting. We ordered beef burgers, fries and beer.

Deepali kept talking and I kept ignoring her. After an hour or so, we went towards Marine Drive, sat there and smoked cigarettes looking at the sea and the blinking ship lights. We were quiet, not talking to each other.

Deepali broke the silence. "Aarush, I want to tell you something."

"I am all ears," I said.

"I think I am falling for you."

I laughed. "Falling where, Deepali?"

"In your shadow, perhaps? You make me challenge myself. I feel that god has sent you into my life for a reason."

"Maybe you are right, maybe you are not. Why waste your time thinking about it?"

"Aarush, I have a mind and I am allowed to think. Don't tell me what to think."

"Deepali, you are a nice person. I hope you grow and reach the peak that nobody ever has. Whatever good or bad happened in your life is for a reason; embrace it, and make the best out of it."

"See, that is the reason I am falling for you. You make me want to be a better person."

"Deepali, I am not who you think I am. I am miserable, boring and sad, living a life in the past. And I have some really fucked up issues to deal with."

"Why don't you share all this with me?"

"I am fine this way. I have issues nobody can ever understand."

"Are they more fucked up than my own issues?" she asked, and as I looked into her eyes, I gulped some more wine and lit another cigarette, trying to break the restlessness building between us.

"I don't know, but I am not able to resolve them for sure," I said.

"Aarush, let me be a part of you. I want you to use me. I want you to be selfish with me. I want all that."

"I am not that guy, Deepali. My issues are mine. I don't want anybody else to be a part of it." I said, looking at the waves colliding with the stones.

"Aarush, look at me," she said, and turned towards me. I looked into her eyes. She said, "Aarush, I love you."

"Deepali, I have nothing to say, nothing to express. I am fucked up, I am insecure and I am a loser. You don't want to be with me. You will get bored of me one day, and then you will leave."

"Maybe I will, but how are so sure about it?"

"Because I know you, and I know myself. We both are alone, and need someone to take care of us, but this does not mean that we are in love. We both are just trying to survive and that is why you are sitting here with me."

"Aarush, let's go back. I want to sleep," she said.

In the room, Deepali did not want me to leave her. I told her, "Deepali, you don't want to be with me. I have to go."

I crawled into my bed, thinking of what Deepali had said. My heart was incapable of believing her. Moreover, I had no feelings for her. I had no feelings left. The door had been closed long ago. She had no idea who I was. She just liked me because I had helped her in some tough situations; not because of who I was, but how she liked to see me.

I was mentally incapable of satisfying her needs. She was way up the ladder and I had yet to climb the first step.

The Contract

$\mathcal{N}$ext morning in office, Suchita ramped over me, calling me an asshole for ditching her on Saturday.

I apologized, telling her that a friend from Delhi had arrived without prior notice.

"Shut up, you asshole. Next time you dare ask me to go somewhere, I will slam your head in the wall," she said, and left.

She was really angry. Maybe this was what betrayal was all about, I said to myself. I started work and after a couple of hours, went down to treat myself to a smoke. As I walked out, I noticed Deepali entering the building of the VP Production Head. Without noticing me, she walked straight into the building.

Meanwhile, Suchita came running towards me, saying, "Now you are not even going to call me for a smoke."

I was irritated. What was Deepali doing here? On top of that, Suchita kept ramming question after question at me and I kept nodding my head like an idiot. And then I asked Suchita to shut up.

She looked at me, and asked, "What's wrong? Why do you act crazy all of a sudden?"

"I am thinking something and you are fucking my head," I told her.

"All right, give me a cigarette. I will go and smoke on the other side."

"No, it's okay. I am sorry."

"Fuck off, Aarush," she said. Then she stood there and said, "Do you know that the director has finally planned to stay in Jaisalmer? Well, check your mailbox."

I smiled. "I will, and what about the crew? Is everybody leaving a day prior?"

"Yes, we all are. You should be ready. He is going to make you cry like a beggar on the set."

"Let him try. I will show him what 'Kahani Humari Tumhari' really is," and we both started laughing.

After half an hour, I got a call from VP Production. "Aarush, come to my office quickly. There is something I need to discuss." I went rushing towards his office.

He introduced me to the lady in his office. "Aarush, meet Ms Deepali."

"Hello, Ma'am," I said, my face poker-straight.

The boss said, "Aarush, please have a seat. Ms Deepali is Marketing Head, Hindustan Lever, our lead sponsor for 'Kahani Humari Tumhari'. She is here to renew the contract for the next six months. Can you please take a dictation from her, and revise the contract so that the formalities are cleared. Both of you can have a seat in the conference room. I will join you in some time."

I looked at her. She looked at me. I smiled, but she looked rather serious, behaving like a total stranger.

"You never told me you were here for this," I told her once we were in the conference room.

"You never asked me what I was here for," she smiled.

"I did, and you said for work. A little detailing would have helped."

"I know. I wanted to see the look on your face."

I grinned. "Well, how do I look?"

"Same, nothing different."

"Whatever, don't play these games with me. I am too old for all this," I said.

"If you are old, then I am probably on my death bed," she said. And we both laughed.

"Can we talk business now?" I asked her.

"No," she said. "We will talk business later. I will ask your boss to fix your meeting with me at night, so that we can spend some time professionally. I want to see your professional side," she said looking towards her vibrating cell phone, with tension in her eyes.

I responded, "You can try whatever you want; the ball is in your court."

"It has always been in my court, you just don't want to see it."

"I like a woman with power, Deepali, but I hate it when any human being challenges my intelligence. So don't push me."

"I will. Let's see what you are capable of."

"Fine, you are going to witness a different side of me, ma'am!"

We stepped out of the conference room. As we passed the lobby, I could see my colleagues looking at me with curiosity.

❖

It was nine. I was sitting in the restaurant at the Lalit, waiting for Deepali to arrive. I had two copies of the contract in my hand.

She walked in through the door, an ethereal vision in a black sari. My eyes popped out. She was looking gorgeous. It took me a while to notice that she had a companion with her. She introduced him, saying that his name was Ranbir.

"So Aarush," said Deepali, turning towards me, "Mr Suresh had said that you will be taking us through the guidelines of the contract."

We ordered drinks, and then Ranbir asked to see the revised contract. He got busy in going through the guidelines. He turned to me to ask a question, but Deepali intervened, saying, "Let him do the talking, Ranbir, and let's do the listening."

I said, "You know the last contract was for the time span of two years, which will get over in a month. As per the previous contract, the sponsorship was for five crore rupees for the term of one year. This included your brand logo at the opening template, the ad cuts for three-four minutes depending upon the duration of one episode, and ending template. Prior to the contract, your sponsorship was for the duration of two years and the TRP rating were varying between 4.5 to 5.5., plus, the viewership ranged between fifty to fifty-five lakh per episode. The viewership on YouTube came as bonus for your company." I said confidently, and saw the two of them nodding.

"In the past two years, the viewership has extended to seventy to eighty lakhs and our current TRP rating is 8-8.5. We are expecting the viewership to grow to about one crore in the duration of two months, and our TRP to hit 9.

Also, on our YouTube channel, we are offering you exclusive sponsorship. In this revised contract, the duration of the ending and starting template may remain the same. So this is what I propose…"

As the talk got over, we ordered dinner.

Ranbir said, "Aarush, once our lawyer goes through this contract, I think we will be free to fly back in two days?"

Deepali said, "Even it takes three days, I don't think it is a major issue for us."

"I will get it ready in two days. I don't want to waste your time. After all, time is precious for us all," I told them.

"Aarush, you talk smart. What are you doing in a production house? You should be handling sales."

"Thank you for your kind words, Ranbir, but I chose this profession after putting a lot of thought into it."

"Are you mesmerized by the glamour that the entertainment industry brings?"

"It is much more than that, Ranbir. I have a plan and all I am doing is trying to stick it out. It sounds a little unconventional in my head as per the norms of the society, but I have never liked anything easy."

Ranbir smiled. "This is good talk to keep you motivated."

I said, putting my fork down to look at him, "That is all a person can do. You've got to justify your actions, not to the world but to yourself."

"Isn't this a defence mechanism, because of psychological warfare in your head?"

"I am very clear in what I am dealing with, and I hope I make it till the end."

"You will. I wish you all the very best."

All this time, Deepali sat quietly.

Finally she said, "I would like to have something sweet. Let's order a honey cherry pie. I have heard that you cannot control yourself after the first bite."

After the dessert, I bid goodbye to both of them, and they went towards the lift lobby.

On my way home, I called Deepali. "So, was I able to sell you the contract in a fair manner or you are still not convinced?"

"Well," she said, "you are just the same as others."

I laughed, "Ranbir has a different perception of me. Both of you were sitting there. If I was not convincing enough, how come you did not say anything then?"

"I had no intention to act as a bad cop out there."

"Fine, have it your way. I am getting bored of this game. You are just upset because your ego was cut down into tiny pieces and then served on a platter for dinner tonight," I said, and hung up.

Man, that was rude. I need to mind my tongue sometimes, or people will stop talking to me someday, I said to myself. Then I thought, let them think what they want. I am not really fond of bullshit either.

The next day, I was busy getting the logistics sorted. My phone was ringing, e-mails were rushing in from train vendors, ticket vendors and hotel vendors; everything seemed to be going on at the same time. It had been only two-and-a-half months and I hated my work profile.

In the evening, Deepali called, inviting me over to her room. When I entered, she was wearing a bathrobe and her hair was wet. There could be no other explanation; she was looking for sex. I held on, however, waiting for her to take the first step.

I lit a cigarette and sat on the sofa. She poured some wine and we both sat down talking about life. She told me that she had schooled at Maharani Gayatri Devi in Jaipur, then graduated from St Stephen's in New Delhi. She had done her MBA from Narsee Munji, Mumbai. I finally understood her background.

I said, "So you know Mumbai in and out, don't you?"

"Yes, of course. I did my post graduation here."

"Then why have you been behaving as if you know dog-shit about Mumbai," I asked her.

"No specific reason. I like it when somebody else takes the responsibly of deciding the places to visit."

"You make me sound stupid. You enjoy playing with my head."

"Sometimes I do. It makes me feel good about myself."

"Well, I am glad I can make you feel good, even if it is because of my sheer ignorance."

She tried to explain herself. "Don't take it that way. I just have difficulty disclosing things about myself. I have been independent ever since my husband died. I like it sometimes when I don't have to use my head. You make me feel easy; I am comfortable in my skin with you."

"Why are you making it difficult for me, Deepali? You are leaving tomorrow evening. I don't know when I'll get to see you again…"

"Aarush, don't fuck your head because of me. Let's talk about something else."

"I think I will play some music," I said to her.

I attached my cell phone to the music system. Whenever I played the game of seduction, I switched to Donna Summers' 'Love to love you, baby', and it always worked.

Deepali was playing with her hair. I walked towards her, made her stand up, and started kissing her neck. She held me tightly from my back, moving her hands up and down. She grabbed my ass. I kept on kissing her neck. Then I dimmed the lights.

She sat on the bed and I pushed her and then went up on her. The music was getting intense and so was our session. I removed her bathrobe and she removed my shirt. She starting licking my nipples and I moaned a little, and let her mouth do the magic. I went down on her and started to lick. Her body went out of control and she started moving uncontrollably on the bed. I told her to relax; it was getting difficult for me.

"Grab my hands," she said. I grabbed her hands, and kept licking her.

After five minutes, she said, "Aarush, fuck me like this is the last day of my life. I cannot take the teasing anymore."

I got out of my jeans and rubbed my manhood on her. I thrust inside her and started ramming her with all the strength I had in my body. Her moans were so loud that I had to put my hand on her mouth. She came on top of me and started moving in swift motions, circular and then angular. I was moaning loudly; I had never had such an experience.

Then she got off and started to suck me like a girl licking ice cream. I closed my eyes and let her do the magic with her mouth. She kept eating me and I kept moaning. She stopped after a while, gulped a glass of water and got into doggy style. I quickly got up and fucked her hard.

After some time, she was exhausted, and I began massaging her thighs. She looked semi-conscious and I tried to relax her. It had been an intense encounter.

In the morning, she was still sleeping, and I ordered an omelette and coffee for both of us. I just had a couple of hundred rupees in my pocket, so preferred not to pay the bill and woke her up.

I kissed her on her cheeks and said, "It is time to see the sun, Deepali."

She mumbled something and went back to sleep, so I wrote her a note as I left: "You are delicious. I wonder why a woman like you is wasting her time with me. Have a good day."

As I entered my office, the director called me to his cabin. He was smoking his pipe, and his bald head was shining like a twinkling star. I told him that we were done with all the logistics. We were done with lighting set-up as instructed, the art properties, hotel and travelling was taken care of. Also, two OV vans would be there during the time of shoot. We would be taking the cameras from Mumbai.

Jaisalmer and
Delhi Again

Last semester exams
23 May 2012

"Ridhima, you can drop me at Rajouri Garden," I told Ridhima. It was late evening. We had just completed our exam, and were on our way back home.

"No, I want to drop you home," she said. "You always drop me home. I should also get a chance to do the same."

"No, Ridhima. I don't want you to drive back home alone. It's getting dark."

"No, I will not."

"Stop it, Ridhima. Don't behave like a kid. Please drop me here."

But she would not listen, and dropped me home. Getting out of the car, kissing her goodbye, I asked her to call me every ten minutes, so that I would know where she was.

After ten minutes I got a call from her, telling me that she was at Netaji Subhash Place.

"Fine," I said. "Let me know once you reach Punjabi Bagh."

After half an hour, however, I received a desperate call from Diksha, Ridhima's sister. "Aarush, do you know where Ridhima is?"

"She is on her way. She must have crossed Punjabi Bagh by now," I reassured her.

"I don't know, Aarush, please find out. She called me up and said she had met with an accident. There were many voices in the background, and I could not really understand where she is and now she not responding to my calls."

My heart stopped beating for a while. "Jesus Christ! Do not worry Diksha, I will just call her and see where she is…"

I called Ridhima, but she did not answer.

I called Diksha again and told her I was on my way, that I would find her car somewhere around the Punjabi Bagh flyover. Diksha said that she would also leave for Punjabi Bagh immediately.

I drove my car towards Punjab Bagh like a fire brigade on alert call. I saw Ridhima's car exactly at the centre of the flyover. I drifted my car onto the left and rushed towards her car. Ridhima's head was against the steering wheel. The front of the car was seriously damaged.

I woke her up. She mumbled, "You have come."

"How are you feeling, Ridhima? Are you all right?" I asked her.

"My head is paining," she mumbled again.

I got her a bottle of water, she gulped it all in one go. I sat with her inside the car. She rested her head on my shoulders. I said, "Everything is fine, baby. Don't worry. Do you want to see a doctor?"

"No, I am okay," she said, talking a bit more clearly now. "There is some pain which will go away…"

When Diksha and her father arrived, we left the car at the accident spot and rushed her to the hospital. Doctors took her to the Emergency to check for internal bleeding. The good thing was that she was conscious. I sat with her, without leaving her hand. I was dead scared, although I knew no severe damage had taken place. My fear was born out of thinking what could have happened. I kissed her forehead infinite times and she rested her head on my shoulders.

She said, "I am sorry, Aarush. You had to come back here. I have damaged the car too. Papa will be angry with me."

"No, he will not be, don't worry. He is your father, and is more concerned about you than anybody else."

I was at Jaisalmer Fort with the team, for the shooting, and I had been thinking of my time with Ridhima in 2012. I brought my mind back to the present.

We were all on the roof and the entire city of Jaisalmer could be seen from the height we were at. The sun was bright, and we had to place reflectors to minimize the lighting on the set. The cameras were placed on the four corners of the roof, and one GoPro camera was stationed with the help of the drone, on the top.

The director called out, "Lights, camera, action!"

The actor shot the actress, and she fell on the floor. The fans helped us to create a required storm. The director called out, "Cut it!"

He had got what he wanted in the first take itself. I was shocked, considering the fact that he liked to piss his crew. How was he satisfied with the first take itself?

We started to dismantle all the equipment. I went in the dining area where we were supposed to take the next shot.

Suchita came up to me. "Aarush, how much time will it take before we are ready for the next shot?"

"An hour or so," I said.

"Okay, I believe I should get the costumes ready."

"Yes, you should," I told her, and looked at the set. We were supposed to place a dimmer light on the top of this huge dining table, but the light man was not able to give a proper angle to the light. I tried to explain it to him, but in vain. So I took the initiative to climb up and adjust the dimmer. With one leg in the air, and one on the ladder, I was trying to reach the knob to adjust the lighting frequency, when I lost my balance and felt straight on the dining table, followed by the ladder. I was badly hurt. My nose started to bleed and my left hand was severely hurt. I could not move.

The director came running towards me, and said, "Aarush, put up your head high in the air to stop the bleeding!"

Suchita came on the scene and called one of the drivers and we left for the hospital.

At the hospital, I told Suchita, "Tell the producers not to let my family know about this. I don't want them to panic for no rhyme or reason." The doctor gave me three stitches on my head. I was in pain, but it was bearable. Suchita looked tense, but I was nonplussed.

"Process of life, Suchita...accidents happen."

"Who told you to climb that ladder, moron? It is not your job." The doctor asked me to keep quiet so we both sat silently, and the doctor kept on stitching, like a designer working on his clothes.

Image shots of Ridhima's accident that took place at the end of the semester exams were moving in my mind. I wanted to call her and tell her that I had met with an accident, but I had lost the guts to do that. I knew what her reply would be.

I was dying of pain on my bed alone. I got up and got myself a pain killer, and I asked god to come down and tell me what wrong I had committed in my life that there was no one around me when I needed somebody to pamper me.

Why couldn't I be happy? Wasn't this what I was supposed to do? I was just doing my job, wasn't I? Fuck it, I knew nobody was going to give a reply. I kept on crawling on my bed, crying in pain and misery.

Around four, Suchita called to check on me. She said she was not able to sleep, so was coming to my room; we could order some coffee or tea. After five minutes, she knocked on the door, and then came and sat on the bed. She said, "You should not have climbed that ladder…"

"Well, there are lots of instances that are not supposed to happen, this is one of them."

"Whatever, just be cautious next time."

"As you say, madam," I said.

We both lay on the bed, and I dozed off to sleep. She was not there in the morning when I woke up in immense pain. My hand was not moving. I managed to get up, came out of my room, and went straight to the hospital to get an x-ray.

"Minor hairline fracture. We need to fix your bone and bandage you," said the doctor.

"I will not get a bandage, doctor, please suggest something else," I told him.

"You have to, or else your bone may stay permanently like this," he said.

I told him I did not care and I came out with a broken arm.

I went on the set and the director called out to me, asking about me. I told him about my hairline fracture.

"Will you be able to manage the work today, or do you need a day off?" he asked.

"No, I will try to manage. If not, I will go back to my room," I said.

"Fine, then don't sit here talking to me. There are many things that need your attention."

It had been a hectic shoot and my only sources of survival were painkillers and cigarettes.

I managed to get a three-day off after the shoot and decided to spend some time back home.

Nikhil was at the airport to receive me. He said, after greeting me, "Bhai, you look miserable, how much weight have you lost?"

"I don't know, man. I am scared to check my weight," I said.

"Bhai what about a gym, have you not joined any?"

"Nope, time crisis," I shrugged.

"Fuck it, you tell me what is going on? And what happened to your hand?"

All is good. Oh, the hand? I fell off from a ladder while while fixing a light."

"That was expected from you," he said.

"I want to do something that is not expected from me, Nikhil."

"And what is that?"

The pain in my hand had started to increase. I started looking for the pills and said, "You tell me."

"I will tell you, if you have the heart to listen to what I say," he said.

"Shoot." I was talking in monosyllables.

"Stop fucking your head, man. Enough of this nonsense! Ridhima is your past. Don't fuck your future and your present because of her."

I had no words, I knew all this, but did not have the strength to admit it.

"I am not fucking myself; I am on the verge of fucking this world in and out."

"I hope you are," he said and he escorted me to a cab.

Though I was happy to be coming home, the several memories that I had been trying to run away from started haunting me.

I tried to get out of them, and started calling my friends and family members. I wanted to see them all, not because I really wanted to, but I guess this was the only way through which my emotions could be kept in check.

I called Nikhil, and asked him to meet me in the evening to go to Karim's, for I was dying to eat some mutton korma and chicken stew.

I sat and had lunch with my family. They were really happy to see me. My mother has made her best dishes.

"Aarush, why don't you eat? What is wrong with you?" she said, looking worried. "I think you should come back. You can find a job in Delhi. It is not like you are not going to get any…" I could see her lips moving in sync but all my attention was diverted towards my shirt sleeves, and I was hoping that she would not notice my swollen hand "

I replied in a very casual tone, "I don't want to come back, I want you to come to Mumbai. Let's all move to Mumbai. Once I get settled there, I will take everyone with me."

My father said, "We are old now and we have no intention to leave our home town."

"As you wish, but I am not planning to come back to Delhi. There are a lot of things that I have yet to do in Mumbai right now."

After everyone had left, my mother looked at my hand. But before she could say anything, I told her about my plans to meet Nikhil in the evening, and that I was fine.

When I met Nikhil in the evening, he told me I needed to trim my beard and look more presentable. I told him then that I was planning to quit my job. I felt I had achieved everything that I was supposed to in this company, and that it was time to come out of my comfort zone. Then I really spilled the beans to him.

I said, "Nikhil, I need to tell you something. I think I am seeing someone."

He was immediately interested. "Who is she and what is up with you two?"

"Her name is Deepali, she is working at Hindustan Lever and is older than me."

"You always wanted to be with an older woman."

"Yaa, I wanted to sleep with one, not date one."

I had a smug look on my face while Nikhil seemed to be bursting with curiosity.

"Then why are you dating her?"

"I don't know what is happening. We are having sex quite frequently, that is for sure."

"Make me meet her. I want to see the fish you have caught."

I called Deepali, "Hi, I am coming to see you in half an hour!"

She was surprised. "When did you arrive in Delhi? You don't even have the courtesy to call me."

"I am coming to meet you, isn't that sweet enough? And I am hopping in with my friend, so be on your best behaviour."

"I am always on my best behaviour, you are the one who does not control your tongue," she said.

"Fine, we will both try to be nice today," I said, and hung up.

When we arrived at her residence, Deepali opened the door with a smile and hugged me. I introduced Nikhil to her. She asked us to sit, and then she went towards the kitchen to fetch something for us to drink.

I whispered to Nikhil, "How is she?"

"Dude, she is fucking hot! How the hell did you manage to get into bed with her?"

"Shut up man! I am not as lame and dumb as I look."

"You are definitely not."

Deepali returned with some French fries. She noticed my hand and asked me what had happened to it.

"I fell from the ladder while fixing a light," I told her.

"Oh gosh, how bad is it?"

"As bad as it looks."

"You could have called an electrician," she said, coming up to me and looking concerned.

"I was fixing a light at the shoot in Jaisalmer. It is your money. I got to do justice to it. It is because of you I broke my hand."

"Don't put it on me. What is the doctor saying?"

"He says I need to bandage it for fifteen days."

"Then where is your bandage?" she asked, looking shocked.

"It is with the doctor. I told him that was not going happen."

"Shut up, you are getting it bandaged tomorrow."

"Good joke, Deepali, but this is not happening. I feel handicapped with a bandage."

"If you will not get it done, you will become handicapped for sure," she warned.

"It will get fixed on its own."

"We shall talk about this tomorrow."

Nikhil intervened, "She is right, Aarush. Don't put your ego into it. Get it bandaged."

I was irritated by all this. "Stop acting like my parents. I am a grown man."

She came and sat a little close to me, "Let me have a look. God, it's swollen like a fat man's tummy!"

"Isn't that good, considering how thin my body is?"

"It may be thin, but you definitely have stamina," she said.

I smiled. Nikhil understood what she was referring to, and preferred to lower his eyes. I lit a cigarette.

For the very first time, she commented on it, "Why do you smoke so much?"

I hated it when anybody commented on my smoking. "I don't know, people call it an addiction," I said.

And we ended up sharing the cigarette and talking about how music in the eighties was much better than in the present.

After dinner, we left, and driving back, Nikhil asked, "What is going on between both of you? She definitely likes you."

"How are you so sure?"

"When a woman likes someone, her eyes show it all."

"Ya, you are right. But I don't know. She is a gorgeous woman, but my head is not straight. I cannot think of anything right now."

"Are you attracted to her?"

"Definitely."

"Then what is holding you back?"

"Life is holding me back. I don't have space for the emotion we call love," I told him point-blank.

"Shut up dude! Why have you become so sad? Do something with your life. Stop acting like a moron, will you?"

"I cannot make you understand my situation, Nikhil. Let destiny decide what is in store for me."

Next morning I found that my hand had swollen and was paining tremendously. I managed to get out of my blanket and look for a painkiller.

After ten minutes, my mother entered my room. "Aarush, it's time to get up. You have to go to the bank, and also to the Pune University office, so get up now."

I stepped out of bed and she noticed my swollen hand. "How did this happen? When did this happen? Did you meet with an accident?" She bombarded me with one question after another.

"Maa, it happened in Jaisalmer. I fell from a ladder."

"What were you doing climbing ladders? Are you a spot boy?"

"No Maa, I was trying to fix a light."

"Are you an electrician?"

"Maa, please. I have seen a doctor. There is nothing to worry about. I am taking painkillers. It will better in a week."

"Stop lying to me. We will go to the doctor right away," she said.

"Maa, I have already seen a doctor."

"No, we are going to the doctor."

My mother finally managed to get my hand bandaged. I had no strength left to protest.

The next evening, Deepali picked me up because I told her I could not drive.

At the Thai restaurant, I said, "I don't feel like drinking today. I am scared I will become an addict."

"So am I," she said. "Then what should we do? Let's have our food, and then maybe watch a movie?"

"I don't want to go back late. I have a bandage on and my parents will start eating my head if I return late."

"Fine, then we will just have dinner and I will drop you home. Are you scared of your parents, Aarush?"

"No, not at all. Why would you ask me this question?"

"Because it sometimes appears to be so," she said, shrugging her shoulders.

"No, I respect them, much more than I love them," I said.

We went to Ricos at Kashmiri Gate, to get the 'appetizer of the day'. Deepali looked at me, her eyes searching my face. "What is the population of Delhi?"

"Around two crores."

"Out of population of two crore people, why did I bump into you that night?"

"Which night?"

"The night I almost ran over a man with my car."

"Probably because I am one of those few idiots who drive around at odd hours at night?" I said, with an arrogant laugh, and looked at her. Seeing her confused was very rare and I was getting cheap pleasure out of her facial expressions.

"But why did I go out that night for a drive?"

"You were frustrated and needed some fresh air, probably that's why?"

"Chuck it," she said, her voice petulant, "you are not getting my point."

"I don't want to think about it. I know what you are pointing towards."

"Aarush, you are talking immaturely right now. Please don't do that. I expect to have an adult talk with you. You have always behaved like a grown-up. Why this sudden anxiety about not talking about what is cooking between us?"

"I am not sure about us. I have yet to climb the ladders of society, and you are already on top. I need time to reach where you are, and during this entire duration, there may be insecurities, drama, worries. I don't think we both have the energy to go through this."

"Don't speak on my behalf; talk about yourself."

"Deepali, I have dealt with this before. It has hardly been eight months since I broke up and I am still not sure whether I am over her or not."

"Fuck you man, all this after seven months…"

"Well, we never really had a conversation about it and you know, I am not comfortable sharing my inner conflicts," I said.

"I was wrong. You don't see me the way I thought you did. I am just a miserable woman for you who is looking for affection and attention."

"Deepali, please, look at my face." I forced her to turn and look at me. "Do you see anything about it? Doesn't it reflect a story of sadness, betrayal and anger? Don't I look tired to you?"

"Aarush, I know what's hitting your head. It will keep on hitting you for a very long time. Get used it, or you may end up losing much more than you already have."

"I know your words bestow glory and truth, but I am not ready to absorb them. Please, I don't know what I am up to, so don't you think it is better that we stop discussing about what is happening between us?"

"If this is the solution, then why not? But how long are you planning to run away from reality?"

I hung my head. "I don't know, I don't know anything."

"Fine, Aarush, take your time. Take as much time as you need."

"Thank you, Deepali. I know it is difficult for you, but it's the same for me."

She dropped me home. We shook hands and she left. Uncertain of what this conversation meant, I was scared to let her go, but even more scared about what was happening with my life.

Return to Mumbai

My mother started crying when I was packing my bag to leave for Mumbai. I touched her feet and whispered in her ears, "I love you, Maa," and left for the airport.

I searched for the keys to my room in my bag once I reached. I looked at the room and thought, "Fuck, I hate this room. How am I going to make anything good in this room? But I hate myself even more for not being able to conquer my fears."

I called Ridhima and she answered my call after the twelfth time. "Why are you calling me, Aarush? Isn't it clear enough that I do not want to talk to you?"

I began to plead. "Ridhima, I am not well. I think something terrible is going to happen to me. I have lost it."

"So what can I do? Go and see a doctor, just don't disturb me, please!"

"Just talk to me for ten minutes, that's all I am asking."

"No, I don't want to talk to you or see you, or even think of you. You are my past."

"Ridhima, please don't talk like this. Why are you behaving with me in this manner?"

"Aarush, I am hanging up. Don't you dare call me back!"

I started to cry and held my head in my hands. I threw the pillow and started crawling on the floor. Why was I dying for her attention, where was my self-respect? I got up from the floor and went to my bed again to rest my hurting head.

I went to the kitchen, got the knife, and started cutting the edges of my bandage and then tore it apart. My hand started to pain again, although after doing this I felt better in my head. I laughed and laughed loudly, telling myself that I was just a stupid fellow, nothing more, nothing less.

There was a note on my desk the next morning: *Not in office. Hope you are doing good, see you tomorrow. Love, Suchita.*

I messaged her, *I am good. Wanted to see you today... anyhow will catch up tomorrow.*

I left for the editing room for the post-production of 'Kahani Humari Tumhari' maha episode.

In the evening, Suchita messaged me to meet her and a friend at the Taj. As I entered the lobby, I saw both of them standing at the entrance. Suchita had a bottle of whisky in her hand.

Suchita said, "The night is just getting younger my friend, it is just getting younger," and we headed to my room in her friend's car.

In the car, I asked Suchita, "I have heard rumours that you're planning to leave the company?"

"Ya. This not my calling, I belong somewhere else," she said.

"Where is that somewhere?"

"Movies maybe, or a documentary. I want to make a documentary of my own."

"What sort of documentary?"

"On the culture and demography of Rajasthan," she said.

I was all ears. This was a very different side of Suchita that I was yet to discover.

"That is an interesting idea," I said.

"Fuck the idea, let's go somewhere…"

"Where?"

"Let's hop into Bar Stock Exchange."

We finished the bottle on the way in the car and entered Bar Stock Exchange. We checked the counter; Red Label was available for eighty rupees! My eyes popped out. I called in for one large Red Label, and they both ordered Jack Daniel's. The music was loud, and the women were hot. Suchita was drunk by then. Her friend soon left, saying, "I have to leave, guys, my roommate is waiting at the door. He does not have house keys with him."

Suchita was talking to me, "Women out here are hot."

I agreed. She asked, "Which one are you eyeing?"

"I don't have the energy for this," I said.

"C'mon, Aarush…don't be a spoilsport."

"You see, I learnt a long time ago that when you are sitting with a girl, don't let your eyes move someplace else…"

"Wow, that is sweet. Do you find me attractive?"

"You are like a gem, a precious gem. A pearl if you are to be named. I don't know if I can afford one."

Suchita leaned over. "For you, I will come for free any day, any time."

"What do you like in me?" I asked her.

"Your eyes…they are so expressive, and the way you talk… they attract quite a crowd."

I was stumped by her words. "Are you serious?"

"Haven't you noticed? It has been only three months, and everybody is to the left and right of you; everybody likes you."

"They just feel safe with me. I am not competition for them. Every person I talk to ends up giving me some advice, of how this industry works, and the mantras for survival in Mumbai."

"Because they all like you. I have never heard anybody bitching about you, and you know how often it happens in our office."

"Maybe you are right. But let's keep the conversation focused on you," I said.

"Tell me anything," she said, leaning over some more. She was awfully drunk.

"I will, but let's leave from here. I have had enough of this music."

We took an auto to my room, picking up a packet of cigarettes and another bottle of whisky. As we entered my room, she went crazy, and started singing something from the Beatles. I followed by singing songs by Red Hot Chilli Peppers, after which we both dozed off to sleep.

When I woke up the next morning, I went to take a shower and then woke her up. She got up within fractions of a second. I asked if she was okay.

"Yes," she said, "just a bad dream."

"What did you dream about?"

"That there are people surrounding me, and our director is shaving my head, and they are laughing and making fun of me…"

"Fuck, that is a scary dream. That bastard! That is certainly a nightmare."

She then made some omelettes for both of us and then she left, saying she would see me in office.

A month later, Deepali was back in Mumbai, but she never bothered to call me, and my arrogance did not permit me to take any initiative.

We were sitting in the conference hall, being formal and polite to each other.

She said, "I came to hand over the cheque, and to get the final contract done. I have received the final invoice, but there were some problem with the audit, so my accounts department had to intervene, and the cheque got delayed. So now I am here to deliver the same."

"That is kind of you, but we could have sent somebody in Delhi to pick up the cheque. Anyhow, thank you for your personal favour."

"No problem, Aarush. I will leave now."

I escorted her to the valet parking. She left in her BMW.

I thought to myself, "What the fuck just happened? That was the most formal conversation I had with anybody in my entire life."

I rushed towards the Vice President's room. "Sir, I hope you know Ms. Deepali was here to personally deliver the cheque."

"Yes, Aarush, she met me before you," he reassured me.

"Sir, is everything okay? How come she came to Mumbai just for this?"

He looked at me. "It sounded weird to me as well. She said she wanted to discuss the documents with me, so my secretary gave you a call."

"Fine sir, thank you for your time."

"Aarush, wait, considering your last interaction with Hindustan Lever, I want you to handle the documentation with Pepsi as well."

I thanked him and walked out. I was still puzzled. If she had come to see me, why didn't she say anything of the sort. What the hell, it was not like her.

In the evening, the moment I stepped out of the office I called Deepali. I said, "Deepali, I know you are angry with me, but if you wanted to see me, all you had to do was say it."

She said, "Misconceptions, Aarush Mehta, misconceptions. I came to drop the cheque, no strings attached."

"So you don't want to see me again?"

"I don't know," she answered.

"I am sorry, Deepali."

"Sorry for what, Aarush?" I heard her voice soften.

"Sorry for being me."

"You cannot help that."

"I want to see you, Deepali. I want to see that face and those eyes and that smile that makes me spin right around..."

"Don't be cheesy. I cannot be angry with you for that long."

"I know, that is what I like about you," I said.

"I am at the Lalit."

She was inviting me over.

"I want you to see my little palace. Can you come?"

"Do you have underwear lying on the floor?"

"Yes, and also jeans, shirts, cigarette butts and books..."

"No way am I entering your kingdom. I am a queen. I will not leave my cave."

"Fine, ma'am, then I will be there."

"How long will you take?" she asked.

"Open the door, close the shutters, order coffee, and I will see you before you're done."

She was playing with the curtains when I entered.

I had bought roses for her: red, yellow and white. I went up close to her and apologized.

"I am sorry for my mistakes and I am here for my punishment, my lady."

"Shut up Aarush. I wish I could speak the way you do."

"Oh, that requires effort and experience. You are too young for it. Give yourself time…"

"Fuck you and your sarcasm," she said, and I had a loud laugh.

She said, "Take me out somewhere."

"Fine," I said, "as long as you foot the bill, I am okay to go on a world tour right away."

"All right, drinks are on me. You take care of the food," she said.

"I am not that hungry."

"Fine then, you pay for my food," she said, and headed for the door. We left in her BMW. The driver kept looking at me in amazement. He must have been wondering how an idiot like me got to share the back seat with her.

We went to Bar Stock, but it was too crowded, and the music was bad so we drove towards Hard Rock Café. As we entered, we got ourselves two shots of tequila, and then ordered two more shots; then two more. 'YMCA' was playing and all the bartenders were on the bar counter dancing.

I got up too, so did Deepali, and we danced to the song. She was crazy and wild, really crazy; she kept on dancing and I let her go crazy. I could see she was happy, and by god she was.

As we reached her room, she asked me to come inside, and we banged the door behind us. In no time, our clothes were off. I asked her where she got all this energy from, and she said that I brought it out in her. And we fucked and fucked and that's all we did the entire night. I left in the morning.

The next evening, I went straight away to the Lalit to see her and we left for the airport.

"Aarush, where does this take us?" she asked, resting her head on my shoulder.

It takes us a long way… far, far away. I am going to miss the wild beauty," I said, stroking her hair.

"I am going to miss you, madman," she said. And we hugged and kissed and she left for my hometown, a place that was far behind me in physicality, but in my head I was still living in the shades of my past.

I took an auto for Versova beach, got myself a bottle of port wine, and sat there looking at the waves.

Somebody had told me once that nothing lasts forever, and that nothing stays with you. It is you and only you, who can make a difference. I wanted to gather the strength to take the right path, and be the one who does things right.

Jaipur

1 Feburary 2015

Twenty days before my break-up with Ridhima, we were at Café Coffee Day, and it was around 9:30 p.m.

I was fairly excited about our third anniversary which was on 22 Feburary.

I had planned a small trip to Jaipur, and wanted to tell her about it.I checked the time on my watch and said, "Hey, I have to reach office by ten."

Ridhima nodded. She said, "I know, we will leave in ten minutes."

I smiled at her and asked her, "Do you want to go to Jaipur on the 21st of February?"

She said, "Is it necessary to celebrate our anniversary this time?"

I was stumped. "Not for me, but aren't you excited about it?"

"I am, but don't feel like doing anything special," she said.

I could not hide the fact that her answer had upset me. "What is up with you? Something is wrong, terribly wrong. You are not behaving like the girl you used to be."

"Aarush, you know everything. Nothing is going right. All aspects of my life are screwed, and screwed big time," she said.

"Ridhima, losing patience is not the answer to it. You may not have everything that you aspire for, but there are many aspects of your life that are right," I told her.

"Aarush, it's nonsense that things turn out all right. At the end of the day, it all remains the same, and you have to learn to deal with it."

I gave her a searching look. "Your thoughts represent sadness, disappointment and anger. Don't be this person. You are better than this. One fine day, the sky will be blue, and there will be birds chirping all around, and you will wake with a smile, a big smile on this beautiful face."

She frowned. "I hope it happens, although I am prepared for the worst."

"Ridhima, I wish I could do something to make you feel better, but my hands are tied; there is nothing much I can do."

"You are getting late," she said, "we should leave."

"We'll leave in five minutes," I said.

We sat for five minutes without saying a word.

Finally I said, "Give me your hand."

As I held her hand, she said, "I am not able to feel anything, no happiness, no sadness…"

I laughed and kissed her on her forehead. "I love you, Ridhima, and we are going to go to Jaipur for sure. I will make you feel a lot of things there."

We left the coffee shop and said goodbye to each other. I left for my office, but I had somehow sensed, that this was the lull before the storm.

Next day, she went for an interview to Radio Junction, where they had called her for an internship vacancy. She called me to say, "Aarush, I think they selected me for the internship!"

"Wow, that's great, Ridhima. Congratulations!"

"I don't know if I am happy or not," she said, sounding uncertain.

"You will be happy in some time. When are you supposed to join?"

"Tomorrow. I don't know whether this the right move or not."

I reassured her, "You do not have anything else to do, so this has to be the right move for now, at least."

"Ya, it seems right at this moment."

"Fine, I am on my way back home, I will talk to you later."

"Okay, see you. I love you," she said.

"I love you too."

And now I was sitting at Barista, the coffee shop below office, enjoying a coffee with Suchita. And she was telling me that she wanted to go to Jaipur.

"I want to see the city. I want to see the place and also the outskirts of the region. After all, if I want to make a documentary, I better start researching."

"When are you planning to go?"

"I don't know, perhaps around the 21st of Feburary? It is the ideal time, neither too cold nor hot. Seems to be the perfect time to visit the pink city."

"Will you take me along? I can easily fit into a suitcase," I joked.

"Yes, you can come along. After all, I need somebody to help me research."

"Fine. Then, will you pay me a stipend?"

"No, but I can offer you an internship. You can work for free with me, and get nothing in return. How does that sound?"

"More cruel than your intentions."

"Yes, I will use you and throw you away in a dustbin," she said and grinned.

"Then the dustbin better be made of gold. I am expensive trash, you see."

"Fuck you! But on a serious note, would you accompany me?"

My head whirled for a second. The 21st was my anniversary with the woman of my life, but then I looked at Suchita and said, " I will go to Pluto with you, if you asked me."

"Great," she said, and then we marched our asses towards the office.

On 21st Feburary, before leaving for the station, I wrote a long e-mail to Ridhima.

Ridhima,

I know the ship has sailed. I know you are long gone. I know whatever has happened is nobody's fault. You and I were supposed to be together like two bodies sharing a soul, and a memory that may last forever and ever. You know I loved you.

This is obviously a very big misunderstanding. You have moved on and I don't really know whether I have too. But I have definitely yet to reach a level where I can maintain peace with you.

I don't know whether I should say these things out loud or not, but you have been living with nothing but misunderstandings. I never had a problem with you socializing. This is the last thing that I would want you to not do. And even smoking, I was okay with that.

Jesus Christ, how do I even begin. Do not make promises that you can never fulfill. You stopped smoking, and once your friend asked me how I had made you quit smoking. Till then I was completely unaware that you had quit smoking for me. I really got an ego boost that day. I thought this woman will do anything for me. I was mesmerized by your guts. I used to pretend to go to sleep during our early conversations on the phone, because when you thought I had fallen asleep you would still talk to me, and say the nicest things about us, and I really used to wonder 'how does she do this?'

I was so mesmerized by everything you used to do, and boy, there is no better feeling in this world when somebody does not want to leave your hand for even a minute! I was so awestruck by everything about you that falling for you was the only option. I ever had. You seemed so perfect to me. Everything you were doing was making me blind, and I just could not look beyond you. But slowly and steadily, everything started fading away.

You started smoking again, and my moment of pride was gone. It was never about you smoking or not smoking, I never asked you to quit smoking, (I just said I do not want my girlfriend to be a smoker), and never in my life have I asked you to quit. And why would I, when I smoked myself, but you did stop smoking... and then after a long time started again. And ever since, it was not about you smoking or not, I only wondered where was the girl who was willing to quit it for me? I have been trying to find the same girl who hugged me so tight once that shivers ran down my body.

And yes.Your Facebook friends! I am sorry, but you were from a girl's school. I was just curious how did you know so many guys, being in a girl's school? I was not insecure. I did not feel that you had broken my trust. But yes, when you made a new Facebook account... that sent me some weird vibes. And even more when you wanted me to have your password! I never wanted to invade somebody's personal account, and so I failed to understand why you were desperate to give me your password. That is why I did not want to give you my password, because I wanted you to trust me and I wanted to do the same. Had I been insecure, I could have checked your phone all the time, but I never did, did I? But sometimes I was curious and I did check, because I wanted to know who were the people in your life. Trust me, that was not insecurity, just curiousity. But you made me feel bad about doing it, so I stopped.

I am sorry, but all this time, I was just trying to find the same girl who held my hand saying she would never leave it again. Maybe she is lost somewhere, I don't know, but somehow I feel she is still there. That is what has made me act crazy all this time.

Anyhow, I know it's over for you. But I am still the same guy, and you are still the same girl, and it has always been about us…the rest is just noise.

And I will wait, not for you, but I will wait for 'us'. So if you feel anytime in your life that we can go back to being innocent and hopelessly in love again, then talk to me. I know it's worth it.

Happy 21ˢᵗ to you.

Bye

As I hit enter, I wondered where had I got the guts to say all this to her from. I knew nothing good would come out of it. I would die of anxiety today, and then tomorrow I would have to get up again and act normal and smile, like everybody does, wearing the mask that the society expectes us to wear.

After this, I called Suchita and asked her to meet me at the railway station. As we sat in the Rajdhani coach S3, I received a message on my phone,

You need to come out of the bubble. It will never happen again. You better maintain peace with it or you will end

*up hurting yourself again and again. PS: Don't e-mail me
again, never ever!*

I looked up from the message and asked Suchita,
"Suchita, are we carrying any alcohol with us?"

"You talk like an alcoholic. Shut up and go to sleep! I
have to scribble our plan of action on arrival and do some
research, I am a little busy."

"That is not the answer to my question."

"No, I don't have any."

"Which berths are ours?"

"The top and middle berth,"she said.

"Fine, I will rest my ass on the top berth; you concentrate
on your work."

"I thought you were accompanying me to offer some
help."

"Right now, I need to help myself...only then I will be
able to help you."

I dozed off to sleep, and woke up around midnight.
Suchita was in deep sleep. I went to the washroom, lit a
cigarette and looked in the mirror. The sound of the train
running on the rails was pretty evident in the background.
I was having a hard time looking into my eyes. I was not
ready to face myself for chasing a woman who had given me
nothing but agony.

I came back and woke Suchita up, telling her I could not
sleep.

"Aarush, when will you stop fucking you head? This is
not right. I am sure this is because of a woman."

"I know all this, Suchita, but somehow my heart is not
willing to accept the fact that she is gone."

"You are sitting in a train with a girl who cares for you, who likes you. All you need to do is divert your energy towards me. I am sure better than your ex."

"Your are better than most of the women I have met, but it is not the same with you, and the fact that you are trying to cheer me up makes me hate myself even more."

"All I can say to you is that it is your life, and the choices you make will stay with you for a long, long time, so you better choose wisely."

"Thank you. Can you sit with me till I go to sleep?"

"Ya, sure," she said.

Arriving at Jaipur, we kept our bags in a hotel room.

Suchita told me that we were first going to Jaigarh Fort, then to Amer Fort and then to the City Palace. At night we would be going to the Birla temple. She had arranged a guide, who would take us to all the places, show us around, and then drop us at the Birla temple.

As Suchita came out after a bath, I could not fail to notice her hair – long, black and wet. She looked ravishing, but I failed to gather the guts to compliment her. As we walked out towards the restaurant, she wore black Ray Ban army glasses, and my heart skipped a beat.

"Suchita, those make you look hot," I told her.

"I know, that is why I wear them," she looked at me and grinned.

We took a cab and left for Jaigarh Fort, where the guide was supposed to meet us. After a hectic afternoon of sightseeing, the guide dropped us at the Birla Mandir.

The white ceilings and the white pyramid surrounded by white lights had a different aura, their own special aura. We went inside and there were foreigners and Indians, jumping and humming tunes of 'Hare Rama Hare Krishna!'

I said, "Suchita, I want to sit here for some time."

The chanting of the hymns was getting louder and louder. I closed my eyes, and all I could hear was 'Hare Rama Hare Krishna, Krishna Krishna Hare Hare!' The tempo was picking up pace and all my energy was focused on the chanting. I took Suchita's hand and we both stood up and started clapping our hands.

Hare Rama Hare Krishna, Krishna Krishna Hare Hare.

And then we started jumping and becoming part of the group. 'Hare Rama, Hare Krishna' was all that echoed in the temple and we kept jumping. Our jumps were getting higher and higher, and my smile was getting brighter and brighter, as I held Suchita's hand.

As the hymns receded, we returned to our conscious state.

I asked Suchita, "What was that? I have never felt anything like this before."

"I have experienced this before. The hymns have the energy to raise your adrenalin. How do you feel?"

"I feel good. Do you believe in the presence of god, Suchita?"

"I certainly believe there is somebody looking at us from somewhere, who has a remote control in his hand."

I was sitting there on the shining white marble floor and I said, "I think that somebody with a remote control does not like me."

"You are wrong. Plus, why would he hate you?"

"That is the question I am going to ask him when we meet."

"He is going to slap you for asking this question."

"Then I am going to slap him back, for trying to control my life," I said.

"Aarush, don't have so much hatred for god. After all, he is within us."

"If he is within us, then I want him to come out and let me be me. I am tired of him bullying me."

"Aarush, you say weird stuff, I don't like you," she said.

"Nor do I, and sometimes even I feel that people should not like me. After all, my thoughts go against the thinking of society, and society wants me to behave in a way that is apparently civilized and decent. Fuck them all in and out."

"I think we should leave; you keep losing it every now and then."

"I am fine, Suchita. I am just asking questions that nobody has answers to. So they all say, you better don't ask those questions or else we have to doubt ourselves, and they hate me for making them doubt themselves.'

We left the temple. All the happiness from the jumping and chanting the hymns was gone, and I walked out the same confused, miserable Aarush that they all say I am. After reaching our room, we ordered dal-roti, and started making notes of what we had seen that day, and how would it help Suchita in profiling the documentary.

I asked her, "Suchita, what is the theme of your documentary?"

"That is what I am here for. All I know is that I am fascinated by the rich heritage and vast barren lands of Rajasthan. The way the women still carry water on their heads for miles and miles, for example, is something to watch and learn from."

"I wish you all the very best, Suchita...you will do wonders in your life."

When we returned to Mumbai, and took separate autos from the station and left for our respective rooms. As I walked passed my room, there were clothes, cigarette butts and bottles lying on the floor. I entered my kitchen and I saw red ants marching in sync, carrying food towards the pipeline connected to the sink. I came out and started looking for the mosquito repellant spray, when my eyes spotted my black bag.

I opened it to see some old pictures and gifts. They represented my memories of the past. There was a perfume bottle and two ink pens, a notebook, a key ring and a tie. I hated them all. I always use to tell Ridhima that we should not exchange gifts. They were supposed to make us happy, but in the long run, they were nothing more than a liability – you could not even get rid of them or throw them away.

I thought, "Dammit! What should I do with these now?"

I called Deepali, and when she told me she was busy, I asked her to sms her address. I wanted her to keep this safe with her. And I couriered my hidden box of old memories to Deepali.

I messaged her, *I have couriered you some personal stuff, hope you will keep it safe. It is precious to me.*

As I entered the office the next day, one of my colleagues, Rishabh, came running towards me to inform me that Suchita was leaving the company. I told him that I knew it.

He was surprised. "Then why didn't you try to convince her to stay?"

"Who am I to convince anybody? She is a grown up girl. She can take her own decisions."

"But Aarush, whatever she is doing is out of a fragmented vision. She does not have a constructive outline, and where will she get the capital for the documentary. She does not have a team... and she hardly has any experience of direction. After all, she was the last assistant director of 'Kahani Humari Tumhari'.

"Rishabh, you and I are not alone in thinking about the odds. I hope she sails through it and grows way ahead in her life."

Suchita came out of the VP's cabin and went straight away to her desk and started packing all her possessions. Everybody noticed her actions and looked at each other out of curiosity, wondering what had just happened. She put her things inside a box. Then she walked up to me to tell me that she was leaving.

"How do you feel, Suchita?"

"I am hoping and trying to remain positive, as I neither have the money to afford my apartment in Mumbai, nor enough to sustain myself for more than fifteen days."

I felt tongue-tied. But somehow I managed to say, "Life always throws challenges at us; it is up to us how we deal with them. We can either bow our heads or face whatever is in front of us."

"I know, Aarush. I will try and make the best out of it."

"Just make sure you do not overlook the motivation behind this major step and get stuck again in finding the luxuries that the world wants us to have."

With that, we both laughed and hugged each other.

As I returned to my desk after seeing her off, I asked myself, "She has the spunk to follow her dreams, then where are my guts? I mean, I want to be a writer, then what the hell am I doing here learning production?"

My heart said, "Hold on, you are not ready for this. You are not as strong as she is. Embrace it and maintain a treaty with it."

I had often felt like roaring out loud from the office rooftop, to all those who thought our life was way better than theirs, "No, you guys are wrong. We are as stupid as you are. We are just sitting at a desk and pretending to be happy."

Later that evening as I entered my room, I started looking left and right, and thought it was all nonsense; it did not make any sense to me anymore. I did not want to live here anymore.

I told myself, "Aarush, it is time to go back. You have experienced whatever you had to."

And so I called my father and told him that I was returning to Delhi. He said, "Don't be stupid, no need for you to come. Spend some more time in Mumbai, only then you will have a better future in Delhi."

I got angry and hung up the phone.

I called Deepali, telling her of my intention to return to Delhi to pursue writing seriously.

Deepali said, "Don't behave like a kid. It may sound easy inside your head, but what you are saying is not practical. Please don't talk crazy.We will talk about this tomorrow."

I got angrier than I already was and hung up again.

I called Nikhil and told him, "Bhai, I am coming. I want to become a writer."

He said, "If you want to become a writer, then start writing in Mumbai itself. What is the point of leaving your job and coming back to Delhi?"

"But, I cannot concentrate on writing while working here."

"You always have some excuse or another. Don't be stupid. You are lucky that you got a job. Now you be smart and stick your ass out there."

I hung up the call. Karma, mother of all excuses.

I lit a cigarette, followed by another. I said to myself, "Aarush, nobody takes you seriously, nobody ever has and nobody ever will. Don't fuck you head over it."

Delhi Again

$\mathcal{A}$ month later, I stepped out of an Air India flight. Nikhil was standing at the arrival counter, and I asked him to meet at the baggage belt. He had access to the inside of the airport, because he had been working with Air India for sometime now. Delhi airport seemed different this time. People looked happier, everybody was smiling. I greeted Nikhil with a smile and we both hugged each other.

He said, "Aarush, you look as pathetic as ever."

"Nikhil, how come you look so mature and smart today?" I asked him, grinning.

"The uniform brings it out of me, man," he said.

"So Air India has inculcated discipline in you?"

"No, I am a different person now. I feel different. I talk differently, and I see differently."

"Shut up, Nikhil! Just take me towards the smoking room. Let's smoke a cigarette before we leave."

Nikhil asked me about the number of days I planned to be in Delhi. He said, "I have an off this Sunday, let's sit and drink rum. Winter is around the corner."

"Yaa, let's see if I get time, then definitely this is going to happen."

"You never take out time for me. We are meeting on Sunday for sure," he said.

"I will try my best," I said, and we both started to walk out of the airport, looking for a cab.

Nikhil gave me a long look and said, "I miss you, bro. I wish I could tell you to come back, but I am certain that you are better off in Mumbai."

"You are right, Nikhil. I will come back when I am ready."

"Ready for what?"

"Ready to face my past."

"You sound like a loser, and this is not you."

The cab had arrived, so getting into it I said, "Nikhil, I am not a loser. I am just fucked up."

And I left for the place where my parents lived. As I entered the house, they were all sleeping. My mother opened the gate for me, rubbing her eyes, and then hugged me tightly. "Aarush, I am so happy to see you!"

Soon everybody came out. We all sat at the dining area, and to me they looked old and sad. My sister came rushing and hugged me, "So you are back! How is Mumbai treating you?"

"Mumbai is treating me the way it is supposed to," I said.

"What does that mean?" She could not understand me.

"I am fine, behen...everything is good. I want to sleep now. It is late, we should all sleep."

"Ya, you should go to sleep."

When I woke up in the morning, I found that my room looked different. The table was gone. There was a landscape painting on the wall opposite the bed. My dartboard was gone and a cloth hanger was fixed there instead. I looked up at the ceiling ot find that the colour was now blue instead of white.

I went out to ask mother about these changes. She said, "Aarush, you don't live here anymore. I thought we could make some adjustments."

"But it is still my room. Why would you take it away from me?"

"Aarush I am sorry. We never thought it would make any difference to you."

"Well, it certainly did. And that is why I am asking you why you would do this?"

"You are here for a couple of days only. Don't fight with me."

And like everybody else, she also ignored my thoughts and feelings. I banged the door behind me and went out to smoke a cigarette.

As I entered the park, I saw the same children roaming around, people walking and trying to lose weight, regain the lost stamina, and maintain their youth. I sat on the bench, lit a cigarette, and called Deepali. She was in office.

"When are you meeting me?" I asked.

"Are you in Delhi?"

"No, but I am planning to fly back. I want to see you."

"No need, concentrate on your work. I will come to Mumbai soon."

She had taken the urge to surprise her away from me, and I was feeling stupid and miserable. "Deepali, you don't miss me, right?"

"I do, but I am not stupid to ignore everything and not let you concentrate on your work."

"Fuck off, you don't want to see me. I am just another guy for you."

"Think as you want."

"Fine, but I am in Delhi. If you have the time and feel like meeting me, let me know, or else you know there are other fish in the sea…"

"If you use these words once more, you will see a shark coming towards you and then you will realize that the hunter is about to get hunted."

"Whatever, I am busy now. I don't have time to see you."

"Fine, then I will come to see you. I want to meet your family, and tell them what kind of a boy you have been."

"Well, okay, you can try that."

In the evening, I went to meet Deepali. I was neatly dressed and had sprayed Ridhima's perfume all over my body. I knocked on Deepali's door and she looked fabulous like always. I could hear 'Rocket Man' in the background. Deepali hugged me and kissed me at the door itself, and I kissed her back. She took my hand and led me towards the living room.

I looked at her and said, "I thought we were going out, why aren't you dressed?"

"I am dressed. This is what I am wearing today. You don't like it?"

"I don't care what you wear, as long you are willing to spend time with me."

"I am here with you," she said.

At the restaurant, as we sipped our drinks, she said, "Aarush, I miss you. It is not easy to wake up in that bed alone all the time."

"Why don't you get transferred to the Mumbai office?" I suggested.

"Do you want me to?"

"I don't know. Do you want to?"

"I know you are not ready for it."

"Pre-conceived notions are termites to any healthy relationship. How can you be so sure about my wants and desires?" I asked her.

"Well, it's written on your face," she said.

"Shut up, don't try to justify an invalid point."

"Fine, don't get angry. I am sorry," she said.

I kept quiet for two minutes. Then I said, "How you are so sure about something? You may be right at times, but not every time. Isn't it better to ask?"

"Whatever, will you please relax?"

"I am leaving, Deepali. I think today is not the right day for us to talk."

She was angry now. "Stop treating me like a fool. It is always you who decides when to meet, where to meet. I have a mind and it does work. I am not a bimbo!"

"When did I call you a bimbo?"

"Well, considering the fact you are always dictating to me what to do, what not to do. Isn't it obvious you think I'm a bimbo?"

"See, again a pre-conceived notion. Thinking you are a bimbo or anything else is certainly not true."

"Whatever, Aarush. I think you should leave."

"I think so too," I said. And I stormed out, furious and agitated.

I thought to myself, "They are all stupid – nothing more, nothing less. And women have come into this world to make me feel stupid. I am certain about it now." I sat in my car, infuriated, and then drove straight to Ridhima's house. Her car was parked right underneath her balcony.

I got my baseball stick out and banged her windshield with it twice. It broke into pieces. I walked towards my car with anger in my eyes. The security guard came running towards me. I showed him the stick and he took two steps backward. Then I got inside my car and left. Towards a place which I was uncertain of. I just kept driving and driving without thinking. It was only after reaching NH-8 that I realized I needed to go back home. That eased a little bit of my anger.

Next morning, I called Deepali to say I was sorry, but she did not answer my repeated calls. It was Saturday, and she would be at home, so I sat in my car and drove towards her house. When I knocked on the door, nobody opened it. I knocked again and again and after ten minutes, a guy came to the door and answered.

I was shocked. I felt as if I had invaded an alien territory. He told me Deepali was at home, but sleeping and invited me in. I just gave him my name and left. I left puzzled and astonished.

I waited for Deepali to call me. She did not call for two days and I left for Mumbai.

Goa and Beyond

$\mathcal{I}$ kept calling Deepali off and on, but she did not answer. One fine morning, out of the blue, I received a call from her. I stood up from my seat and rushed towards the washroom to speak with her privately.

I said, "To what do I owe the honour, that Her Majesty herself is wanting to speak to me?"

"Aarush, you know I love you, right?"

"I thought you did, but it is not the same anymore, for sure."

"I want to tell you something…"

"Of course, or else why would you have bothered to call me?"

"Aarush, I am getting married!"

I could not speak. My mouth froze. I hung up the phone and switched it off. I went inside the loo, and rested for some time. Then I went back to my desk, packed my bag, and left for my room.

I bought myself a pack of cigarettes and two bottles of port wine and entered my cave. I told myself, "It is going to be a long night, Aarush Mehta!" I laughed and kept on laughing, opened the bottle of wine and drank half of it in one go before lighting a cigarette.

I switched on some trance music for a change. After around two hours, I switched my cell phone on and wrote Deepali a message.

Deepali, my best wishes to you and your about-to-be husband. May god be with you both always.

And then I started drinking again and looked towards the wall. There was hardly any light in the room. The fan was moving slowly in a circular motion, and so was my head. I was in an oblivion and as I looked more closely at the ceiling fan, I saw somebody with his head upside down hanging on it. I looked more intently and I could see my face, laughing loudly like a devil. I had a red face, my eyes were sparking black fire, and the hands were pointing in my direction. So I made a jump and tried to pull myself down, but somehow I managed to escape. And so I went to the kitchen and got the broom and tried to hit the ceiling fan with it, but I was not willing to come down.

I became more frustrated with the laugh echoing in my head, and I rushed towards the shaving mirror and removed it from the wall and threw it on the fan with all my energy and force. The pieces of glass came back at me, my hair was filled with them and I had cuts all over my face and hands. I tried to remove some of the broken mirror pieces from my hair and got more cuts instead and my hands were covered in blood. I managed to open the gate and started searching for an auto and found one after five minutes.

"Arre bhaiya, kaise lag gayi itni? Aap kahan lad kar aye ho?" asked the auto driver.

I asked him to take me to the nearby hospital. I was straight away taken to the Emergency and a nurse removed my clothes slowly and steadily. With a brush, she started to remove the pieces of mirror from my hair and my body, then washed my hands, sponged my body with warm water, and said, "Why do you guys fight so brutally? Don't you love yourself?"

I told her, "The wall mirror came down upon me."

She replied, "I see at least ten cases like yours every day, and I wonder why it is always the wall mirror that falls." And we both laughed as she started applying some stinging ointment all over my bruises.

She finally said, "You are free to leave, but it would be preferable if you did not keep a wall mirror at home." On my return, I somehow managed to clean the floor and change the bedsheet. I took a pain killer and then dozed off to sleep.

The next morning, I received a message from Deepali, *Thank you for your wishes, Aarush. You have given me the strength that nobody else could have.*

I looked at the cuts and bruises all over my body. When will I stop doing this nonsense? I asked myself.

I entered my office with the cuts and bruises, e-mailed my resignation to the Vice President, packed my stuff in a box and silently walked out. I went to the nearest ATM and checked the account balance in my card. Available balance: 11,000 rupees!

I took an auto and went to the railway station, checked that the next train for Goa was at 04:00 hours. I waited at the ticket counter for fifteen minutes, and bought a ticket in the sleeper class.

I returned to my room, and packed for the next three hours before I dozed off to sleep.

I woke up at three o'clock in the morning and rushed towards the railways station. I had trouble finding an auto. I walked for a mile, but all in vain. Finally at 3:45 a.m. I got an auto. I told the driver I would pay him fifty rupees extra, if he could make me reach the station by four. He agreed, and drove the auto on the empty streets like a cheetah hunting a deer. As I reached the railway station, I ran towards the platform, and kept running. The train had started, but I somehow managed to jump into the last coach.

As soon as I arrived in Goa, I went to a nearby wine shop and got myself a pack of beer, hired a bike and left for Arambol beach. I took my shirt off and sat on the beach; the sand was hot underneath. I drank while I Googled for escorts in Goa. I found the number of one of the pimps.

I called him and said I was looking for a girl.

He told me he knew many Russians, but I wanted an Indian girl, and he did not know any. I asked him the cost of one of the girls, and he quoted a price. I gave him my hotel room number, and then I sat on the beach and waited for the sun to set.

At around eight, I left for my room. I switched on the television after a very long time. I felt a little lighter in my head and had a smile on my face. I looked at myself in the mirror. I was free. I smiled and smiled.

The doorbell rang; the pimp was at the gate and so was the girl. She greeted me and I said hello.

She entered the room. I paid the pimp, and he told me to use protection. I agreed. Thereafter, he counted the money and left.

I went inside the room and the beautiful woman was sitting and smiling at me. What a smile! She was a tall woman and her hair was blonde and her eyes were black.

I smiled at her and she said, "Would you order me a drink?"

I said, "There is some whisky on the table." She got up and poured some whisky, and asked my name. I told her my name, and she said her name was Nina.

"So how long have you been here?" I asked.

"Am I here for an interview?"

"No, just asking."

"You are really cute, would you not sit with me?"

"Of course."

She came and sat on my lap and said, "Baby, I will take you to a different world. Would you like me to give you a massage?"

"No, just sit here, without talking to me, that's all I need. Somebody to sit beside me, nothing more, nothing less."

"Oh, come on! The night is young. You got to have some fun," she said, and she took my hands and guided them towards her breasts and started moving them in a circular motion. She came close to me and started licking my earlobes. All the sadness started to disappear. She caught one hand and guided it onto her back, saying, "Feel it, boy, feel it." I started caressing her back and she started rubbing her hands on my shorts. Then she took off, went on her knees and started to smell my cock through my shorts. In no time, she removed my shorts and massaged her hands on the already hard dick. I took a loud intake of breath. My head rested at the back of the sofa and I opened my eyes as she took it in her mouth. She had a long face and her tongue made me go weak. It was getting difficult for me to sit in one position. My legs were getting uncomfortable, and I started to moan.

She got up and removed her blue low neck t-shirt. Her breasts popped out, and she started to rub her breasts on my face; and then went down on my cock and started rubbing. She rubbed and I moaned. She had taken over my body and my mind. She knew the act way too well. She got up and said, "Fuck me boy, I am all yours."

I said, "I want you to spank my ass, I want you to enslave me today, woman. I want to be controlled."

She made me stand up and like a little boy directed me towards the bed and then pushed me onto it.

I was on the bed naked, with my ass towards her. She brought her hand and spanked me; I moaned in ecstasy. And she spanked me again and again, and I moaned in pain. She kept on spanking and calling me a loser, and I kept on moaning and moaning. She stopped after a while, then brought her cunt towards my face and sat on it, saying, "Lick me, you fool, lick me." I started to lick her and she moaned, and I licked her some more. And then she got up and I fucked her doggy style with all the force in my body.

I told her, "Pass me the cigarette," and lit the cigarette, and fucked her the way she deserved it. I released my cum on the bed, and rested my head on the pillow for some time. She got up and brought me a bottle of water. I looked at her and smiled; she smiled back.

She said, "That's all you need in your life – fucking. Everything else disappears. Sex makes us happy and I like to make people happy."

"I can see that you are a smart woman. You did your best work today."

"I know I am good. We still have one hour left." She asked, "What do you want to do?"

"Just sit in peace and drink some more, that's all I want to do."

"Oh, come on," she said, and she went down again, towards my sleeping penis, and started to play with my balls. Then she used her index finger and started to rub my asshole, saying, "Do you like it? Do you want more of it?" I could not reply, my mind was already in a different zone and she kept on touching my balls and my asshole, while I sat there, not knowing what to do. She had a control my body and I felt enslaved, and it was a new feeling.

When she left, it took me some time to get back to my senses. I lit a cigarette and took out my laptop and decided to write something – anything, just play with words, to express, to know, to channelize what I was feeling. So I started to type.

Dear Aarush,

I write today to remind you and take you on a journey we call life, to take you on a road that leads nowhere. Aarush, the world is a dangerous place, and we all deal with situations that are beyond the control of human intelligence and body, but that does not mean if one or two situations go wrong, you lose hope and become a total maniac, and rebel against almost every rule that has ever been created for the benefit of mankind. That is not right, and you know that. It is you who has to master your actions and nobody else.

Understand that you cannot control the actions and desires of the world around you, but the only person you can control is Aarush, so you better make him perfect. All the scars and pain that are your life right now will fade away if you want them to. Remember when you were a child what you used to dream of? Follow that dream. Make your life worth living. It is time, know what you were born to do. Write a fucking novel, write a story, or anything worthwhile that's worth your effort. Love your writing and I promise you, you will not be disappointed, and all the smoking and drinking, and feeling miserable will be long gone, and your heart will be pure again. Make sure your blood is being put to good use. Start writing, my friend, the world wants you to write, and you want the world to know you have arrived and in full swing. That every bone and every muscle and every nerve of your body combined together are going in creating a novel. It is okay to be fucked, but what is more important is to never let the spirit die within you. Love yourself, Aarush, the rest is just air; smoke that has no direction. All the best.

The next morning I called Nikhil, telling him I needed some cash to return home, and he sent it to my account immediately.

When I arrived in Mumbai from Goa, I packed all the remaining stuff and couriered it to my Delhi house address, and then took the next flight to New Delhi. Nikhil greeted me. He said, "Bhai, it's time to paint the world red!"

"That is why I am back, Nikhil. I will make Delhi black and white and people will ask who is it who has arrived…"

"Where was all this confidence earlier, Aarush?" he asked me.

"I kept it with myself for some time. I know I am going to unleash the energy I have and write my novel."

"Promise me that I will be a part of your novel."

"Nikhil bhai, you are and always will be my friend. A novel will not define our friendship."

At the smoking room, he offered me a cigarette, but I declined. "I don't smoke anymore, Nikhil," I said.

"Are you sure?"

"I have never been so sure." I looked at him and said, "I feel good today. I feel proud of myself."

"I hope this energy stays within you."

"It will, and it will last till the end of my life."

He dropped me to the cab and I told him, "I will see you after I have completed my first draft, not before that."

"No worries. I will come to see you if you don't."

"Time will tell Nikhil, but let me tell you something... from today onwards, I will decide my own fate."

It was 2:30 at night when I rang the bell. Nobody answered. I rang again, and again, and finally my mother opened the door.

She smiled and said, "What a surprise, Aarush! I am so happy to see you."

I know, Maa. That is why I came back. I have left the job."

Dad came out, and said, "Where did you come from at this odd hour?"

I touched his feet and said, "I came back, Dad."

"We will talk in the morning," he said, and left for his room. I asked Mom to give me some food and she heated some dal and rotis. I felt in heaven eating the food. I had been having so many omelettes that chickens had been haunting me at night, poking me with their beaks in my dreams.

"Dad had made some chicken, should I serve it?" mother asked.

"No Maa. No more chicken. I am a vegetarian now."

She laughed. "I am so glad to see you. I missed you, I don't want you to leave, stay with us."

"I will not go now. I am here to take care of my family," I said.

My mother smiled. I went to bed, but before heading off to sleep, I removed the scenery hanging right in front of my eyes.

Goodbye Deepali

10 Feburary 2015

$\mathcal{O}$n the day before my break-up with Ridhima, I was sitting watching a cricket game on television. Kohli was about to hit a century. Nikhil called me and said he wanted to meet me at the Buddha Bar.

He said, "We will watch the second inning there, I have free passes.We won't need to pay for the booze."

I met Nikhil at the entrance of the bar, and we both entered, cheering "India, India."

We got ourselves centered somewhere in the middle of the crowd. Nikhil went towards the bar to get some beer. My eyes were stuck on Shane Watson. He was on fire; every second ball was being hit for a four, and I was sagging in disappointment.

One more four, to Ravichandran Ashwin, and in utter disappointment, I walked towards the other side. That's when my eyes settled on a girl wearing a pink top, howling with excitement and having shots.

I walked towards her. "Ridhima!" I said. She looked at me, expressionless. I greeted her friends. I knew them and hated them.

"Ridhima," I said, "you said you were in office."

"Well, I wanted to spend some time alone without you."

"So you could have said that. When have I stopped you from doing what you wanted?"

"You cannot stop me from doing anything. You know that very well."

"I have no such intentions either."

"Good," she said. "Then why are you talking to me like this?"

"Because you came out to watch the match telling me you were at office."

"It is crowded inside, can we go out?"

Once outside, I asked her, "Ridhima, you behaviour is getting strange. You said you don't want to meet anybody, and yet you are sitting here, having shots...?"

"I wanted to go out with my friends. Is there something wrong in that?"

"Nothing is wrong, baby, but you didn't have to lie to me."

"Well, I just wanted to see how I feel without you, so I went out."

"Whatever you say. Have fun!"

"Fine, I am going inside," she said, and left.

I called Nikhil and asked him to come out.

When he came outside, he looked at me in surprise. "What happened? I don't want to miss a ball..."

I said, "I am leaving Nikhil. You enjoy the match."

"What the fuck??"

"I don't know. I am not feeling good. I just want to leave."

"Have a beer," he said, "you will feel better."

"No, I want to go back."

I messaged Ridhima that I was leaving, but she did not reply.

After two hours, I received a call from Ridhima. She said, "Aarush, you no longer control my life, you better stop intervening."

"Ridhima, are you drunk? Who is with you? Let me talk to Supriya. How will guys drive back home?"

"I will somehow. You don't need to be so concerned about me."

"Then who the fuck am I supposed to be concerned about?"

"I don't know, just stop portraying yourself as the king of the world."

"Ridhima, you are drunk, don't say all this. Now please tell me how you will return home?"

"I don't know, and I am not even bothered."

"I will be there in a while, you better stay there," I said. Then I called Supriya and told her to wait with Ridhima till I arrived.

When I reached the bar, I saw that she was sloshed. She had puked maybe ten times, Supriya told me, and I saw how she was falling on one person, then on another. I told myself that she was still the same person, nothing had changed; she was still the same. And I lifted her, got her into the front seat of the car, put on her seat belt and drove towards her house.

Throughout the drive, she was incoherent, saying things that I could not understand. Supriya and I led her till the stairs, after which I had to lift her and carry her to her flat on the second floor.

As I left her, she said to me, "Fuck off, Aarush."

I told Supriya to take care of her and left.

The next morning, I messaged her:

Hope you are fine. I love you baby, please don't talk to me the way you did last night. Call me when you are in your senses.

And the next day, she told me it was all over.

One month after my return to New Delhi from Mumbai, I went to my usual haunt, the park in my neighbourhood to write on my laptop. As I entered the park, all the stray dogs came rushing towards me. I got out the packet of biscuits and distributed amongst them equally. They all knew me now. The stray dogs were the only friends I had since the past month. I had been coming here to sit in the concrete hut and look at my blank laptop screen and write; to try to develop a story that may turn my fate upside down.

So far, the only success I had was ten thousand words of a journey. It was getting more difficult for me every day to write, and I felt the same way today. As I stared at my laptop screen, an old gentleman walked up to me and asked me what I was doing.

"Struggling, sir," I said, looking up at him from my laptop.

"Struggling to achieve what?"

"To become a better person. Let the anguish and hatred come out of my system."

"You are too young to say these words, young man. Life is simple. Why are you complicating your life? The whole of the past month, you have been coming and sitting here with your laptop. What are you trying to achieve?" He was asking me the same question again.

"Sir, time will tell, only time and nothing else. I will let time decide whether my actions are right or not. All I know is, I come here with a purpose, and till the time I achieve it, I will sit in this park, look at my laptop and transform my thoughts into words."

"All the best to your stubbornness," he said, and walked away.

I finished writing the last word of the first draft of my novel.

I looked around. Children were playing *gilli danda* in the mud, I got up and asked them if they would let me play with them. It had started to rain, but they happily agreed. I took the stick from their hands, and shot the gilli high in the air. Then we started to calculate the runs scored from the stick. The total distance that the stick takes to touch the gilli is the number of runs scored. It took twenty-five sticks to reach the gilli, which meant twenty-five runs. Not bad for a first timer!

It was the boy's turn now. He smashed the gilli way up, high in the air. We ran to catch the gilli, but missed. We started to calculate the distance between the stick and gilli. He had scored thirty-two runs, so he won. I congratulated him and gave him fifty rupees.

I picked up my laptop and went towards a printing shop to get a hard copy of the first draft, and as the pages were being printed, I was jumping with excitement inside me, which was hardly visible on my face.

I kissed the first draft and walked out, looking straight into the eyes of the world.

One fine morning, when I was working on the second draft, I got a call from Deepali. She wanted me to come to her wedding in Delhi at the Taj.

I laughed out loud and told her I'd be there. I felt like throwing the cell phone away. But then I realized that my throwing the cell phone on the floor would not stop her from getting married, nor would she realize my anger and disappointment.

I obliged and got ready on the day of the wedding. As I entered the wedding hall, the bride and groom were sitting on a fairly big sofa. There were people smiling and dancing and the hall was filled with happiness. Honey Singh's songs could be heard in the background. I was happy she was getting married, but wanted to know why she did this to me, and whether a person deserved to be treated like a puppet. I went on to the stage and greeted them both. She looked really happy. After all that she had gone through, she deserved it.

"Congratulations Deepali, congratulations, my friend," I said, "I wish you both a very happy life ahead."

"Thank you, Aarush," said Deepali and gave me a big smile.

I got myself photographed with the couple and I walked out of the hall. After all, it was an end to a fairly important chapter of my life. I had never wished to marry her. It was today that I understood the difference between attraction and love. Playing Rolling Stones' 'You can't always get what you want', which was the need of the hour, I drove back home.

A New Friend

Almost on the verge of completing my second draft, I found that my urge to smoke was increasing. Wherever I went, I would see people smoking, and I had started to forget why I had quit in the first place. So I got up and went towards the panwadi and bought a packed of Benson & Hedges. I was about to light one when I realized that it was not about quitting cigarettes, it was about resistance and failure. And I kept the packet in my pocket, as a reminder of who I was, and what I aimed to be. I turned back towards the park.

After about half an hour, the old guy who had spoken to me earlier came up to me. I greeted him.

"So how is the struggle going, young man?" he asked.

"Sir, I am still struggling. How can a struggle be good? It is always filled with pain and fury."

"But the end result is not."

"Sir, the result can be anything, I am prepared for the worst." I looked at him; he appeared smart and sensible. I asked him, "Sir, what makes you visit this park every day?"

"I am retired. I don't have much to do, so I sit here often."

"But sir, isn't there anything that you always wanted to do? If yes, then this the time."

"I am too old; my ambitions have died," he said, shrugging his bony shoulders.

"Sir, your soul is still alive, so please don't say that. What do you wish to do?"

"Never thought about it, people don't talk to retired people like us, so we forgot that we are alive..."

"People always forget, sir; they are too self-centered to remember anything. I think you've got to be selfish."

"Maybe you are right, beta. I will think about it today, if there's anything that I want to do. And from tomorrow, I will think about how I can do it."

"Fine, sir, then tomorrow once you are done thinking, please do come to the park. We will sit and see how you can achieve a wish that you could never fulfil during your busier days."

The next day, I was sitting inside the summer house in the park, typing away on the laptop, when Uncle arrived and said, "I have always wanted to learn painting. I think it is time for me to pick up the brush."

"Sir, have you ever painted?"

"When I was in school. At the time, people used to deride painters. They were considered to be of the third category, to which no one wanted to belong."

"Nothing has changed even today. Painters are admired by only a few."

"I know. But I am too old to think about how people will look at me. Nobody really sees me now. I am just an old man and sometimes while walking towards the park, people offer me a lift and that is all they do."

"Fine, then let's make a deal. You will read my book first and then I will find you someone who can help you to paint the painting of your dreams."

"It's a deal. What is your name?"

"Aarush."

"Your parents must be really proud of you, Aarush."

I frowned. "They will be, sir, one day."

"Oh yes, they are, you just don't know it yet."

"Maybe…maybe not. If they are, they've never said it."

The next day, I handed the second draft of my novel to Uncle.

"By what time will you complete reading it?" I asked him.

"Maybe two days?"

"Okay, Uncle," I told him, "take your time."

He laughed and then smiled and said, "Time is the only thing I have in abundance."

And we both laughed.

"Uncle, I never asked you, what did you do before you retired?"

"I was a teacher in a government school. I taught English literature."

"Wow! That is really nice. Why did you leave teaching? There are always students who are looking for people like you."

"I got bored. The Indian system does not allow students to grow. They are limited to moving from one book to another. The practicalities which we all deal with remain unknown to them."

"At least we have reached somewhere. You cannot build a castle in this short span of time."

"No we cannot, and I agree with you. But we are still trying to build a castle that the Britishers wanted us to build; no real effort is being made. It is completely mechanical.

There is no innovation. A structure that Britishers dreamed of is what we are building. If you ask me, they may have left the country, but our brains are still dependent on their intellect and are controlled by their ideologies."

Not many people said what he did. I mean, we knew how westernization had conquered our minds but we were too comfortable living this way.

His thoughts were igniting my already rebellious mind frame. "You are right, sir, I don't think we are ready to accept your thoughts yet."

"I know, but you know, neither am I!" he said. "I have read Shakespeare and forgotten the stories by Rabindarnath Tagore. If you ask me, Tagore is better."

I don't know, sir. I haven't read Tagore. Though I did pick a book of his quotes from the British Council library some time ago.

"I know son, nobody reads Tagore today. I will see you in two days."

Two days later, he prepared some notes for me, and pointed out a chunk of grammatical errors. "It is a good read, but you fall low on vocabulary," he told me.

"But sir, isn't the narrative more important?"

"Everything is important, and if you do not have command over the language, then you will never be a good writer."

"Sir, is it worth a read or am I just shooting arrows in the dark?"

"I don't know, I am a cynical. I don't like anything. Your story is good, but it is not for me. However, I have performed my duty. It is your turn now, to find me a painter who can teach me."

"Thank you, sir. Tomorrow you'll get a call from one of the tutors," I promised him.

The next day, I called him. "I have found a painter, but he will not come to your house; he can teach you painting at his gallery."

"Where is his gallery?"

"Gol market. Let's go together to see if he is worth your time and investment."

As I was driving, Uncle gave me a pen. He said, "It will remind you of me, once I am gone."

"I will remember you...I don't need a pen."

"But still, keep it for me please."

"No sir, I am sorry."

"You are stubborn kid."

"Sorry Uncle, if I offended you," I said, as I parked the car in Gol Market, and started to look for the SFS government flat where Usman the painter had his gallery.

Uncle was a little slow and irritated. He began telling me how the place used to look back in those days when there were hardly any cars on the roads. He used to travel in a bullock cart, and used to smoke a pipe. He sounded like Raj Kapoor of the sixties to me.

As we started taking the stairs, I helped him climb the first floor. "It is going to be a problem to climb fifteen stairs, a challenge in itself," he said, taking my support and climbing one stair at a time.

"Yes Uncle, you have to cross the challenges to learn painting."

"I don't know whether I have this much motivation to learn."

"Let's go to the gallery, and then figure it out."

As we entered the gallery, we saw it was lit up by yellow lights. Various paintings from horses to naked women were hanging on the walls. Warriors and bloodshed, flowers and famines...you name it, he had it. While searching on Google I had found that Usman was a fairly popular painter overseas and his paintings were worth lakhs.

As we were looking around, an aristocratic old man walked towards us. His white beard depicted wisdom and his eyes held fire. I felt a little under-confident standing next to him, as the yellow lights made him look even brighter. I introduced Uncle to him. I had already spoken to Usman earlier about us. Usman looked at Uncle and said, "So sir, what is this sudden fascination to learn art?"

"I always wanted to, but forgot, as life passed by," said Uncle.

Usman asked, "Are you sure, or is it just another way of passing time?"

"I don't know, my friend. Let the brush and the artist hidden within me decide."

"Fine, sir. I am free on Sundays. You can come here after nine in the morning."

"What is the fee?" Uncle asked.

"No fee. God has given me enough. I am hoping to pass my art to others so that art does not die."

"Thank you. In the meantime, can I take a look at the magnificent art around?" Uncle asked.

"Yes, of course," said Usman.

And Uncle and I started looking at the canvases around us, trying to understand how and when one comes up with the idea of painting, to create something that portrays a sense of usualness, but is in itself so unusual.

A week later, I was busy writing the synopsis for my novel in the park when I received a call from Uncle. I told him I was in the park and he came over to meet me. As I watched him entering the park gate, I noticed that he was walking a little faster than he usually did. He had a big smile on his facee and was murmuring something to himself. I asked him how his first class had gone.

"Oh, it was good. Usman taught me how to pick up the brush and then how to swiftly move it on the canvas. Then he taught me the purpose of colours...which colour represents which emotion. He seems like a fairly knowledgeable guy, and we discussed the world over a cup of tea."

"Good to hear that."

"Yes, it was amazing. I bought cookies for you from Indian Coffee House," Uncle said.

I thanked him and then he left. I started writing the synopsis of my novel to impress a publisher to influence him into publishing my story.

The next day, I was preparing the final e-mail to send to publishers who might show interest in my manuscript, when I heard music and I saw Uncle walking towards me, matching his steps to the beat of the song. He was listening to the Beatles. I laughed as I watched him almost dance his way towards me.

"Do you like John Lennon?" I asked him as he came and sat next to me.

"Yes, he is my favorite, and you guys know nothing about him. John Lennon was the best. And his music is far better than the music you hear nowadays, which has no sense, no depth and no lyrics, no pain and no heart. I have no idea what is wrong with you folks."

I said, "Uncle, why are you offloading your agony about every youth in this country onto me? I mean, I thought I was your friend."

"Yes, you are, but you are as young as everybody I see around and as common as them too...I do not see anything vibrant in you too...

He was old and irritated by almost everything that exists in this world, or probably universe. I had to challenge myself that I was better than his words of wisdom, and so in order to not give up I replied.

"Uncle, c'mon! Please don't say that."

"Fine, but you are all lost." He had to have his way.

"Okay, Uncle, as you say."

He asked me then, "What are you working on?"

"I am about to send the final e-mail to some publishers." I looked at him. "Would you like to go through it once?"

"Sure, I am pretty sure there will be some grammatical errors." He took out his black-rimmed glasses from the top pocket of his shirt, and started to read every word aloud, rather carefully. And smartly, with an accent. His accent made me want to laugh, but I resisted. He was very serious about the reading.

After fifteen minutes of concentrating and making some changes, he told me that the copy was ready.

"Is it appealing enough?"

"Don't ask questions that I do not want to answer. Just send this to the publishers."

I hit enter and the e-mail was sent to all the ten publishers in one go.

He said, "All the best, son." I smiled and thanked him.

"You have done a good job, you know. I hope your words come alive for your readers."

"They will," I said, and for that moment, I was very sure.

When I switched my laptop on a week later, there were eighteen rejection e-mails, telling me what was wrong with the story. I yawned. Sending fifteen proposals and getting eighteen rejections was a reward in itself. What a big failure! I had received three extra rejections. That was the strangest happening this morning! I made myself a banana shake and headed towards the gym with a blank mind. After I returned from the gym, I went to the park with my laptop. To my surprise, Uncle was already sitting there. I went and sat next to him.

He said, "So Aarush, you seem rather happy today?"

"I am indeed, Uncle. I just got eighteen rejections, after sending fifteen proposals."

He laughed aloud. "That's good news. It just means all those publishers are not worth your time."

"What do you mean?"

"I mean, find ten other and be prepared for fifteen more rejections."

"Is my writing that bad?" I was upset by his words.

"No," he said, "this is a process. If today you will be disappointed, then your dreams of becoming a writer will remain a dream. You see, the game is not over till last ball has been bowled."

"I know that, Uncle, but nobody can hit ten runs in one ball."

"Yes, because the odds are against it. There is no 'if and but'. You've got to keep trying. And one day if you don't succeed, you can write another novel and title it "The Story of My Failures". It would be an interesting read."

"Yeah, you are right...you are a smart old man," I said.

"I know," he said and smiled. "I just forgot this as time passed by."

"Anyhow, what will I get after losing hope? After all, that is the only asset I currently have."

"See, now you are talking," he said and we continued to chat about this and that.

When he walked away, I sat there and once again started searching for publishers, not only in the Indian, but the international market as well.

It was another cold day in Delhi a week later when I put on my blue jacket and went towards the park.

I called up the old man and told him, "I have two acceptance e-mails. We have to review them."

"It's cold," he said, "and I am not well. I cannot come."

"Fine, take care."

I made the next call to the publisher, "Hello, this is Aarush, could you connect me to Vinita? I am a writer. I sent her my manuscript which she has shown interest in."

I was connected to Vinita, who asked me to come to their office to discuss the publishing details. "Could you come within the next two hours?" she added.

Of course I could.

The Publishers

There was a pile of manuscripts lying on her black wooden table, and she was smoking a cigarette. I could now relate this to why I used to smoke. Every smoker has a deep connection with smoke. That woman had power, and her face was a like a warrior's – blank and ruthless. Without looking up at me, concentrating on her laptop, she asked me to sit. I sat, without saying a word, adjusting my shirt.

She did not say anything for two minutes. Then she slid a copy of an agreement towards me.

It was a little insulting, but I preferred not taking it personally. Then without taking her face out of the laptop, she asked me to go out, read the agreement and then come back. I did so without a word.

A woman came up to me and asked me if I wanted coffee or tea.

She then said, "If there is any query regarding the agreement, you can come to me. I am sitting in the next cabin."

"Fine, miss, I will. Give me some time," I said.

After reading the agreement through, I knocked on Vinita's door. She was still sitting in the same manner. I looked around and realized that the entire interior of the room was black. In fact, her coat was also black, although her skin was white as milk. Getting my eyes off her was a little difficult.

"Aarush, you can talk to Heena; her cabin is next door. Talk to her regarding the agreement, and discuss the details with her. She'll guide you through." She did not bother to look at me as she spoke. I stepped out and stepped into Heena's cabin, for the door was open.

Heena said, "So, Aarush, did you go through the document?" I nodded and she continued, "Is there anything that you have trouble understanding? Anything that you want to ask?" She was full of questions.

"Lots of things," I said. " The advance is a little less and so is the royalty, for one. Secondly, if the book is being sold in the international market, then isn't the cost quoted less than what it should be? Also, I would like to know the public relation strategy that you are planning to formulate. I mean, without PR, this book will not sell. After all, it is a pretty unconventional read."

"Well, in terms of advance, there is nothing much we can do. You are a fresher and we would be investing a lot of money in you. We are not even sure how we are going to reach the market as you are new, and the topic of your book is a little old…"

"Ma'am," I said, "do you think that love stories are a thing of the past?"

"They are all the same, and there is a lot of competition when it comes to romance novels."

"I agree with you, but this does not change the fact that the story is unconventional…"

"Maybe, but it is a risk. And only after contemplating all the pros and cons, we have offered you this advance. However, royalty is something that we can work upon. I have to talk to Vinita and see what she suggests. The PR strategy will come in place once you have signed the contract with us."

"Fine, then, you can talk to her and let me know," I said.

"Of course I will. But that will take some more time. At least have some coffee or tea till then."

And we both sat and had coffee for ten minutes or so, and then I left, my future undecided.

Hidden Truths

$\mathcal{U}$sman and Uncle invited me to the art gallery on Sunday morning. We sat together and Usman began telling us why he had become painter, when Uncle intervened, saying, "Aarush has written a novel – a romance."

Usman looked at me, eyebrows raised, "So I am sitting with a future Booker prize winner, is it?"

"Sir, I will be satisfied if I sell a hundred copies."

"Satisfaction is the death of desire, Aarush," Usman said.

"Sir, you've got to make a choice. Either be satisfied or leave your life filled with desires. I do not want my desires to mess with the peace of my mind."

"I have never met a writer who is satisfied. How come you seek satisfaction in today's world?"

"I seek happiness and balance. Is it too much to ask?"

"You are right, boy, it is not. Come, let me show you few paintings which are close to my heart that I keep hidden from the world."

Uncle followed us slowly as we walked to the room where Usman kept his special paintings. As we entered the room, I could see roughly fifteen paintings. There was no furniture or paint on the walls of exposed red bricks. The room was lit up with oil lamps. This, along with the oil lamps made the room look more authentic and real. The paintings made me feel alive; I felt they were talking to me.

Uncle looked at the paintings and he asked Usman, "Why do you draw so many light houses in your paintings?"

Usman said, "Because there is always someone watching."

"In your paintings or in reality?"

"In reality and in my paintings, both." His words were deep.

"Sir, these paintings speak to me; all these wounded horses, bloodshed of soldiers, the dancing eunuchs and those egotistical pandits chanting mantras, and the unknown light source coming from the tunnel, and the sleeping man on the middle berth of the train filled with human bodies – I can feel the pain in them, how brutally and unknowingly we have sabotaged human beings around us. I wish someday we all understand that there is no possible escape, our karma will someday catch up and the day will come when we confess our lives not to someone but ourselves. I guess these have come out of certain situations that have left a huge impact on you.

"I know, Aarush. They have been in this room for a very long time. I have tried to compile my life in these paintings. I wish that after I die, they keep my dead body in this room. I want to die surrounded with them. Maybe after my death if my dead body is kept in this room, I will come alive."

Uncle said, matter-of-factly, "Usman, you are a good painter, but I don't know if a ghost would be able to paint…"

"You will get an answer once I die."

"Oh, I know I will die before you. Maybe then I will come up to you one day and tell you how it feels to be a walking dead man."

"All right, guys. You guys are scaring me now," I said.

We left the room and headed towards the main gallery.

Usman asked me to stay for dinner.

"We can share some drinks. I want you to narrate your novel to me. I want to see if there is some delicious juice there that is worth my time."

"Sir, I left drinking way back in Mumbai, but I will send you a pdf today."

"You will start drinking again one day. Life does not permit an artist to sit sober for too long."

"Let fate decide, sir, and today is certainly not the day that I will begin."

In the car, Uncle said, "Looking at your face, I am sure you were a heavy drinker."

"I used to drink much, Uncle. After some time, my eyes will be clear again and my face will have its colour back, then your doubts shall be cleared. I really do not drink anymore."

"Okay. But if you drink again, we shall drink together. It has been ages since somebody shared a glass with me."

"Sure Uncle, we'll do that."

And he switched on the radio. I wanted to stop him to tell him that after my break-up with Ridhima, I had not heard the radio. I was scared that it'd trigger any memory that was even remotely close to her.

❖

The next morning, I got ready to meet Heena at the Indian Coffee House, Connaught Place. She was almost done with the editing process and wanted to talk about my work. I called up Uncle and took him with me. When he came over to sit in the car, I noticed he was dressed in a black coat and white shirt.

"Why are you dressed like a lawyer?" I asked him, my eyes mirroring my surprise.

"This is the only coat I have, and I had to look my best. After all, she might be your future wife!"

"Okay Uncle, we are going there to discuss our book, not seek a wedding proposal. I hope you know that."

"Both the things can be done simultaneously."

"Uncle, please don't make me look like a fool in front of her. I do not want my editor to look down upon me."

"C'mon, you are already a fool, I am sure she knows that." He laughed.

And he switched the radio on again. FM Gold, and to my surprise, '*Ajeeb dastan hai yeh*' was being played. Uncle started humming the song, probably remembering his romantic days.

As we reached Indian Coffee House, Uncle asked me how he looked. "You look the same. You are an old man. Her age is the same as your granddaughter's," I reprimanded him.

"But she is not my granddaughter; you just wait and watch my magic."

As we sat down, Uncle began telling me what the Indian Coffee House was like in his days. There were pipes being smoked and the Beatles being played. Ganja and charas was nowhere to be seen. He said, "In those days, people were civilized, sipping coffee and discussing politics using refined language, unlike this '*madarchod*' and '*bhenchod*' that you guys spill out."

Heena arrived, we ordered coffee, and Uncle started interviewing her. "So beta, are you married?"

She laughed and said, "No sir, I am not."

"Do you have a boyfriend?"

"Sir, I don't...it is a little complicated."

"What is so complicated? You either have one or you don't?"

"Sir, I don't know. I am here just to discuss the a chapter of his book..."

I looked down in embarrassment.

"I know beta, but do you like Aarush?"

"He is a good writer, Uncle, and seems like a good human being too."

"Uncle, she is running late. Can we talk about the chapter?"

"Okay, but this is an important discussion. We will do this some other time for sure." And he got up to use the loo.

I looked at Heena apologetically. "I am sorry, he is old and quite bored."

"It is okay. It is good that you have an old man who likes you and cares about you. So I have marked the paragraph in which the father dies. I think it is not relevant in the book. Please go through it once and see if we can remove it."

"Fine, I will do that, but the father had to die."

"Yes he had to, but this does not mean we have to elaborate the entire incident."

"As you say. Let me go through it."

After five minutes I said, "Okay, I will remove this part and send you a revised copy. Apart from this, is there anything that has drawn your attention?"

"Nothing much, only some grammatical errors and punctuation mistakes, which I will take care of."

"By what time do you think we will be able to release it?"

"The first of next month, I guess."

"Great, how do you see the book coming out, Heena?"

"It is engaging. The rest depends on the readers."

Uncle returned, and ordered some more coffee.

Heena asked me, "So what is your plan after the book release?"

"I do not know. I am too intrigued with the release. I hardly have time to think about anything else. What about you?"

Uncle intervened, "Yes, Heena, you should get married now."

We laughed, and Uncle launched into the history of Indian Coffee House again.

The Sun Sets

Two weeks before the press release, I sat with Vinita and Heena in Vinita's office. We were preparing our press release. Vinita was making it hard for me not to have a cigarette, and temptation was at its prime. I asked Heena if she could ask somebody to get me a coffee. She got up and called for some.

Vinita asked me if I was excited. I told her, "I am having sleepless nights. I hope it turns out well. A lot is at stake. What about you?"

"I am not. I have played this game a lot. It will do well. I do not put my hand on anything until and unless it is not a bestseller," she said with absolute confidence.

Heena said, "She is right. She has an eye for a bestseller."

We got busy again. After about ten minutes, Vinita asked, "Do you want a cigarette?"

"I quit a long time back."

"Your hands are trembling, so your body wants one."

"My heart says no, my body may react as it wants," I said.

"Why would anyone quit smoking? What are you so afraid of?"

"I am afraid of losing control."

"Oh, believe me, cigarettes have got nothing to do with it."

"Well, for me, cigarettes have got everything to do with it."

It was ten at night when we decided we would continue the work the next day. We got up and packed our bags and I asked Heena if she wanted a lift.

"Only if you are comfortable with it."

"Not a problem," I said.

Heena said, while sitting in the car, "You know what Aarush, I want to write a book one day. That is why I joined this publishing house."

"Then what is stopping you?"

"It is difficult. I do not have that sense of concentration. I cannot work alone. You see, I am scared of isolation."

"Everyone is scared of going through it alone. But if you make that a reason, you will never be able to write."

"One day, I will surely gather the strength."

"You will, but you know, time is running faster than anybody can ever imagine." Saying that, I dropped her outside her apartment.

It was a week before the press release. I sat with Uncle in the park. I had bought him a new shirt, to wear at my book release.

He said, "Thank you for this, Aarush."

"No problem," I smiled. "I want you to look good. After all, you have been the lighting lamp during this entire process of my writing."

"No, it is you who did it. I am just an old man who is passing time, and waiting for death to arrive."

I was agitated at his words. "Why do you always say that? Don't you want to become a successful painter?"

"No, I just like to paint. I am too old to consider success or any other goal as something to strive for."

"Don't say that! You make me feel depressed with your words. Why do you want me to feel more depressed than I already am?

"Okay, I am sorry."

"No worries. Tomorrow we will go to Indian Coffee House and smoke a pipe. You said it has been ages you smoked one…"

"Yes, that's a good idea, we will."

We looked at the setting sun in the horizon.

He said, "See, the sun has started to set. I don't know how many such evenings I will witness in my life."

I touched him gently and said, "Go back home, Uncle. Your family will be waiting to see you."

The next morning, I called Uncle. A lady answered, in a sobbing voice.

I introduced myself, a bit hesitantly. "Hi, can I talk to Uncle? This is…Aarush."

"He is no more, beta," she said and started crying. I hung up the phone and ran towards his house as fast as I could, chanting Hanuman Chalisa, praying to god that the words I had just heard were not true. I ran and ran as fast as I could.

I asked the watchman at the gate, "You know the old man who I used to drop at the apartment gate? Can you tell me where he lives?"

The guard said, "He died today morning of a heart attack. They have taken the body to Nigambodh Ghat for cremation."

I could not stop the tears in my eyes. I sat right there and started shouting loudly, "Why, god, why...why did you do this?"

The watchman gave me water. After a while, I got up and started walking back home. It was a very long walk towards my house. My sobbing was uncontrollable and of everything that I had experienced in my life, this was the worst. When I reached home, I was stumbling, hardly able to see anything.

My mother came running towards me. "What, beta, what happened?"

I could not speak. I tried to, but I just could not. My sobs were getting louder and louder. My heart was bleeding. I fainted.

After what seemed like a very long time, I gained consciousness and looked around. My mother was sitting next to me, holding my hand.

"Are you okay, Aarush?" I saw the lines of concern on her face.

"Maa, the old man died, Maa..."

"What are you saying? Who died?"

"The old man, Maa, he died." I started to sob again. My entire family stood around me, trying to understand what was wrong. But I had no words to speak; only the tears were flowing.

The next day, my father took me to a doctor. I had not been able to see clearly or listen to anyone. The doctor made me relax on the couch. He gave me some medicine, and after fifteen minutes or so, he asked me about what had happened.

I mumbled, "The old man died. I cannot believe…"

"Who is this old man?"

"I used to meet him every day in the park. He was more of a friend to me."

"Okay, I am prescribing you some medicines for your emotional breakdown. All this crying will not bring any good. You must try to stay calm."

My mother made me some food which I ate with great difficulty, and then I went to my room to try and sleep.

A couple of days later I went to Usman to tell him about what had happened. I entered his gallery and called out his name. Usman walked out with a big smile on his face. "Welcome, come let me show you the painting that I have just finished."

I stepped forwards and said, "Sir, Uncle died three days ago." My voice was breaking.

His face had no expression, as if he knew that it was about to happen. He went inside without speaking a word, and came out after two minutes, with a painting in his hand. "See, Aarush! He was completing this painting. He was trying to draw a sketch of you. It is incomplete. He wanted to paint you red. He said that this boy has shades of red in him – shades of anger."

I looked at the painting and I smiled. I told Usman, "I am happy that I was a part of his life for some time. He came into my life to help me through this writing process. I don't know if god had sent him or not, but I really hope that he is happy, wherever his soul might be."

Usman smiled and said, "Yes Aarush, you are right. I am happy that you are seeing it this way. He was a great guy. He wanted to gift this painting to you. Unfortunately, he could not complete it, but I think you should keep this sketch."

"Sir, he will always be close to me. I will keep this sketch in my room to remind me of him."

"Wherever he is, I am sure he will be wishing you all the very best. Would you share a drink with me today, just as a toast to the old man?"

"Sir, let's smoke a pipe; he loved smoking a pipe. We were supposed to have one together."

And we both sat and talked about him and his life and smoked a pipe. After some time, I came back home with the sketch, and placed it on the wall right in front of my bed.

A New Beginning

My mother woke me up. I opened my eyes and saw the sketch. Mother said, "It is your big day, Aarush. How do you feel?"

"I am okay, Maa," I said, looking at her.

She smiled and said, "Come, get up, you have to go for your book release; your new life is waiting for you.'

I went to the washroom and took a deep look at my face in the mirror. I had forgotten how my face looked. I wore a clean pair of jeans and a white shirt and sprayed the last bit of Ridhima's perfume on myself. I laughed and decided that I had to finish the perfume. I applied more than I was supposed to, and threw away the bottle. From the car keys, I removed the key ring that Deepali had gifted me, and threw that away as well.

The book release was at Pragati Maidan. As I entered the venue, I found that it was surprisingly crowded. A big banner of my book was being fixed on a flex wall at the back of the stage. I could see my family and friends and some strange faces in the crowd. I noticed Heena as I walked up to the podium. I said to myself, "Congratulations, Aarush, you did it! You should be proud of yourself!"

I unveiled the cover of my book.

Nikhil came up and congratulated me. So did everybody else and after I ended my speech and walked down, many other people came up to me. I greeted them all with a bright smile.

Heena came towards me and said, "So Aarush, all's well that ends well."

She was followed by Vinita, who said, "You did a fantastic job. I promise you this novel will take you miles ahead in the game."

I thanked them and went to my parents, touched their feet. Their faces were lit up and my father said, "I am glad we have a son like you." I smiled at them.

As the event got over and everybody left, I went towards my car. When I was about to get inside, I saw a girl standing at a distance calling out my name.

I called out to her, "Weren't you suppose to be inside? What are you doing here, standing in the dark?"

"I was waiting for you."

"Thank you for coming, Suchita. How are you doing?" I said, walking up to her. We hugged each other.

"You did it, Aarush! Much before I could. I am still bumping my head against the wall, trying to raise funds."

"Do not worry, girl. You will make it. I know you will."

"Oh yes, I know I will. But sometimes it seems so difficult."

"Take it from me, if it is getting difficult, then let it stay this away, because as time passes by, you will get used to this chaos and start enjoying it."

Suchita looked at me, eyebrows raised. "So you got the inspiration of writing this book from your ex?"

"Well, you've got to read it. Only then you will have the answer to your question."

"And am I a small part of it?"

I grinned at her. "Maybe, maybe not. You've got to read it, that's all."

"Are there any chances that I can be a part of your real life? To be honest, I am not really concerned whether I am in the book or not."

"You *are* a part of my life. Why are you asking me this question?"

"Because I want to be a part of you. I want to hold your hand and take my step forward in life."

I could not say anything. She continued, "I want to grow old with you, Aarush.

I hugged her again and said, "I am yet to finish my day. I hope you can give me a night or two."

"I understand," she said.

I drove towards Ridhima's house, from where all this had started. It would be better that I ended it there itself. It was dark, but I could see her balcony clearly, standing as I was underneath the house of the woman I had wanted to spend the rest of my life with.

It had been three sixty-five days since the time when I had last seen her smile. The different shades of her smile were swimming in front of my eyes. There had been a devil in her laugh. She had told me, "Do not hate me, but I cannot be with you anymore."

I had felt so weak then, my weakness could not be stated in words. Thinking about that day still sent shivers down my body.

I had died that day and since the past year I had been a dead body, a body without a soul, without any meaning. I started laughing loudly, standing there beneath her balcony. There was a devil in my laugh today.

Had it been Ridhima or somebody else who had triggered the sequence of events, I was still not sure. All I knew was that I was born again and maybe this time around, death would not be as painful. Maybe this time I would be sleeping when Yamraj arrived.

All I could hear was my heart telling me I had to live to die again and again. I had to smile because there were people around me who expected me to smile. I had to be a face in the crowd and play a role that society demanded of me.

The truth is that everybody is dead and very few are able to realize this. She had made me live for a moment or two. She had made me happy for some time. Now it was time to go back to the world where we were all dead and all I could do was thank her for making me live for a while. I was not laughing anymore, but I had a smile on my face. My smile was real, so was I. The time had come to cherish the desire to live and then to die, again and again.

Next morning I called Suchita. She responded in a husky, sleepy voice, "Aarush! It is too early to start the day."

"No Suchita, we are too late. We've got to start it right now."

"Whatever. Let me sleep for a while."

"No, I will not. The day has just started… and so has our life."